THE
FIRST CHURCH

Moving In Series Book 4

RON RIPLEY

EDITED BY EMMA SALAM

ISBN: 979-8-89476-014-8
Copyright © 2016 by ScareStreet.com

This is a work of fiction. Any resemblance to actual persons, living or dead, or actual events is purely coincidental.

Enter the Realm of Terror...

We'd like to take a moment to thank you for your support and invite you to join our VIP newsletter.

Dive deeper into the darkness with exclusive offers, early access to new releases, and bone-chilling deals when you sign up at www.ScareStreet.com.

Let the nightmares begin…

See you in the shadows,
Scare Street

Chapter 1
Doubting Thomases

"Are you sure you heard him say 'ghost'?" Matt asked.

Carlton nodded. "I know I heard him say ghost."

They stood in the alley to the left of Sam's Smoke Shop. The two boys, in spite of only being fourteen, had managed to get Matt's sister to sell them a six pack of Budweiser, but the plan to drink it had been put on hold.

Reverend Joe, it turned out, had to leave the office earlier than usual.

Mrs. Staples, who was supposed to clean the Church, had gotten an emergency call from her pet sitter. One of her cats was stuck in a wall again.

The Church would be empty.

"How did you hear him?" Matt asked, keeping an eye on the Church office. The Reverend's car idled in its parking spot. Their religious leader would leave at any moment.

"It was last night," Carlton said. "I was helping my mom clean up after youth group. She was pretty upset about something and was talking to Dan's mom. When I passed by the Rev's office, I heard him on the phone."

"What did he say exactly?" Matt asked, looking away from the Church, for a moment, and at his friend.

Carlton brushed a stray lock of blonde hair out of his eyes and said, "The Rev said, 'I've got a headless ghost running around the Church.'"

"Who was he talking to?" Matt said, glancing back at the car. It remained where it was. Exhaust slipped out steadily from the tailpipe and into the cold afternoon March air.

"Don't know," Carlton answered. "He said 'thank you' and I had to make like I was texting when he came out. He went right over to talk to my mom and Dave's mom. It was weird. All of them were acting strange."

"Hell," Matt said, "if I'd seen a headless ghost, I'd be pumped up."

"Right," Carlton said with a grin.

"Reminds me of the movie Sleepy Hollow, you know, the one with Johnny Depp," Matt said. He smiled. "Maybe he's looking for his head."

Carlton laughed. "Think he'll try to take ours?"

Matt scoffed and shook his head. "Nah, ghosts can't hurt anybody."

"True," Carlton said.

"Oh snap, the Rev's leaving," Matt said. He and Carlton turned their attention to the man's little black Prius. They watched it back out of the parking space, go in reverse, and head down Main Street.

"So," Carlton said, looking at his friend. "You still have the key?"

Matt grinned. "Yes, I do. Mrs. Staples still thinks Jim lost it after he fixed the broken window in the kitchen for her."

Carlton rolled his eyes. "Kid annoys me."

"Kid annoys everyone," Matt replied. He slapped his friend's thick shoulder. "Come on, we'll cut around behind the Hurlington House."

The two teenage boys moved quickly out of the alley. Matt broke out the beer from his back pack, took a pair and passed one to Carlton. As soon as they crossed the street and made it to the safety of the old, run down Hurlington building, they paused so they could open them.

Each of them winced at the first few gulps, but then, excited smiles all over their faces, they made their way to the back of the Church.

With quick steps, they slipped into the Old Burial Ground, settled down behind the Hanover monument and carefully watched the Church's back door. They waited until they were finished, quickly drank another pair and then left the empty cans in the dirt.

No one came out of the office. The lights remained off.

Matt fished the key out of his pocket and nodded to Carlton.

Together, they stood and walked leisurely to the exit. One last glance around showed they were unobserved. Matt unlocked the door. They slipped inside and locked out the rest of Rye, New Hampshire.

The air smelled heavily of the Rev's spiced tea, and the cleaning supplies

Mrs. Staples constantly scoured the whole Church with. There was enough light from the afternoon sun to fill the office.

Matt looked around. "So, do you think we'll be able to see a ghost, even though it's daytime?"

"Don't know," Carlton said, shrugging. "Maybe we'll have to wait?"

"Maybe," Matt said. He went and sat in the Rev's seat and put his feet up on the desk. "Carlton, we should totally drink the last ones in here."

Carlton laughed and shook his head. "Nah. I'm pretty sure Mrs. Staples would figure it out, she'd smell the beer and then she'd hang us from the rafters."

"True," Matt said, grinning. "Anyway, did the Rev say where he saw the ghost?"

"No," Carlton answered. "I mean, maybe he did, but it would have been before I heard him."

"It's just weird," Matt said after a minute. "No one's ever talked about seeing any ghosts before."

"I thought the same thing," Carlton said, leaning up against a filing cabinet. "You figure someone would have talked about it."

"Yeah, exactly," Matt said.

A creak sounded outside the door which led into the hallway.

Carlton and Matt looked at one another, their eyes wide.

The doorknob twisted to the left and then to the right.

Carlton glanced at the back door, wondered briefly if they had enough time to make it, and then froze in place as the noise stopped.

He risked a glance back and saw he and Matt were still safe.

A form slipped through the wall and stood on the old rug in front of the desk.

It was short, even without its head. A man's body clad in a uniform of some sort. The hands opened and closed, and a question was asked in a language neither of the boys understood.

Both Carlton and Matt, however, took their phones out, pressed the camcorder icon, and recorded the ghost.

Another question was asked, again the words completely foreign, but louder.

"Dude," Matt said, laughing, "this is crazy!"

"I know!" Carlton said. His own laughter joined his friend's, and he stepped back as the ghost advanced towards him. "Man, this is just like Call of Duty! Only, he's headless, and not a zombie!"

"Right," Matt said with a laugh. "This is like the best special effects ever!"

"I am so putting this up on YouTube when we're done," Carlton said. "This thing is definitely going to go viral. We'll be famous! Maybe we can even get our own show on the Travel Channel."

"Careful," Matt said, grinning, "I think he likes you."

Carlton couldn't answer. He tried not to laugh too hard so he could keep the camera focused.

The ghost lunged at him, and its hands found Carlton's head. He dropped the phone as the dead thing's thumbs found his eyes and plunged into his sockets.

Carlton screamed and collapsed to his knees.

Matt realized he wasn't able to run. His legs wouldn't respond, even though he wanted them to move, to get him away. But he remained where he was, watching, as he kept the hideous image of his friend being blinded centered in the lens.

The headless ghost let go of Carlton, and then turned toward Matt and raced at him.

Matt's screams soon joined his friend's.

CHAPTER 2

A MEETING WITH THE REVEREND

Brian Roy sat in the Riverwalk Coffee Shop in Rye, New Hampshire while he waited for Reverend Joseph Malleus. He was on his second cup, because the coffee was actually pretty good. The man had called the night before and been adamant about the arrival of a ghost in his church.

A headless ghost.

Even as a ghost hunter, Brian might have scoffed at the story, if he hadn't recently survived the destruction of Middlebury Sanitarium.

Brian discovered he was now a lot more open-minded.

"How's the coffee?"

He looked up and saw a young woman standing beside his table. She wasn't the waitress who had served him.

"It's really good," Brian answered, smiling.

"Glad to hear it," she said. "My name's Lisa. I'm taking over for Sarah, her shift's done. Let me know if you need anything."

"Will do, Lisa," he said. "Thanks."

Brian watched her walk back to the counter. She was tall, with short black hair and of Asian ancestry. Her white shirt and khaki pants fit nicely on her lithe figure. He caught sight of a dragon tattoo showing out of the collar of her shirt, and in the light of the shop, he could make out the faint outlines of more ink beneath her sleeves.

Brian smiled, took another drink and turned to the door as the bell above it chimed.

A pale skinned, thickset man walked into the cafe. His blonde hair was cropped close to his head as was his slightly darker beard. The man's eyes, which were a strikingly bright blue, darted around the shop.

Reverend Joseph Malleus, Brian thought. The newcomer wore an all-black suit with the religious white collar.

Brian lifted his mug up and caught the man's attention.

The Reverend smiled nervously and hurried over to him.

Brian stood as he offered his hand.

"Brian Roy?" The man asked, his grip strong.

"I am. And you're Reverend Malleus?" Brian said, sitting back down.

"Yes, but you can either call me Reverend Joe, or the Rev," he said. "The kids call me the Rev, and well, I like it."

"Fair enough," Brian said.

Reverend Joe turned slightly in his chair, motioned to Lisa, and the young woman hurried over.

"Afternoon, Rev," she said with a grin. "You want your tea?"

"Yes please, Lisa," he answered. "How's your father?"

"About the same," she said, her smile faltering. "But, thanks for asking. He still won't see anyone but family, though."

Reverend Joe nodded. "Understood. Please have him call me as soon as he feels like he can tolerate my presence."

"I will," she said, and her grin returned. "Be right back with your tea."

"Thank you."

The Reverend turned his attention back to Brian. "Sorry. We're a pretty small community. I try to keep track of everyone."

"Sounds good to me," Brian said. He looked at the man and realized the Reverend would probably avoid the issue for as long as possible. "Why don't you tell me what happened at your church?"

Reverend Joe fidgeted with his wedding ring nervously for a minute. He was about to speak when Lisa returned with his tea and set it down on the table.

A strong, spice smell floated up with the steam from the cup.

"Well," he said, looking down, "the first occurrence was last weekend. Mrs. Staples, who cleans for us, ran into him. Or, it. I'm not sure. The ghost is headless."

Brian smiled. "Let's say 'he' for now, just to make it easier, okay?"

Reverend Joe nodded. "He. Yes. So, I was working at my desk while Mrs. Staples was cleaning the office, and when she looked up, she saw it… him, standing in the doorway. He was filthy, and headless, of course, and her first reaction was to snap at him."

"What?" Brian asked, laughing in spite of himself.

The Rev blushed slightly and nodded. "She's rather a bit of a spitfire. She told him that she'd just finished cleaning and he was going to make a mess of the hall."

"What happened?"

"Well, I just sort of sat there, shocked. The ghost though, he left," the Reverend said.

Brian shook his head and finished his drink. "I'll need to meet this Mrs. Staples."

"Good," the Rev said. "She's already insisted on speaking with you."

"Okay," Brian said, smiling. "So, she reprimanded the ghost, and he left. Has anyone else seen him?"

"Yes. I did again, last night, with Mrs. Williamson," the Reverend said. "We didn't challenge him, though. We left as quickly as possible."

"And you called me," Brian added.

"And I called you," the Rev agreed.

A police cruiser, with an ambulance directly behind it, raced past the front of the shop. The sirens blared, and lights flashed maniacally.

A phone started to ring, and the Reverend took a cellphone out of an inner pocket. "Could you excuse me?"

"Sure," Brian said, sitting back a little in his chair.

"Hello?" The Rev said.

He listened for a minute before all of the color drained from his face as he looked at Brian in horror.

"Yes," the Reverend said hoarsely. "Yes. I'll be right there."

With a shaking hand, he ended the call and put the phone back in his pocket.

7

"Reverend?" Brian asked.

"I'm sorry," Reverend Joe said. "I... well, you see, Mrs. Staples just called. She went into the Church, she'd forgotten her scarf, and she found two boys. Two of our youth group members. They'd gotten into the office... and..."

"Reverend?" Brian asked gently.

The Rev looked at Brian and said, "Someone ripped their eyes out."

CHAPTER 3

JIM GETS READY FOR DINNER

At fifteen years old, Jim Bogue looked like he was twelve. He was too small for his age and too thin. His dad told him that on a regular basis.

The glasses he wore made him look younger.

He'd heard enough Harry Potter jokes to last him a lifetime.

But Jim had inherited his mother's hazel eyes and her father's harsh features.

He had his dad's hair and bad attitude.

His father was away on a deployment to Afghanistan, though, so Jim didn't have to worry too much about the 'gentle' slaps his Dad gave when he had a drunk on.

"James," his mother said from the kitchen.

He looked up from the Star Wars book he had started to read and said, "Yeah?"

"Dinner time, kiddo."

Jim slipped a bookmark in, got up and went into the kitchen. The table was set for three, which meant his grandfather was on his way down. While his mother set a pot roast on the table, Jim took the water out of the fridge and filled all three glasses.

The thump of his grandfather's cane on the stairs sang out loudly.

Jim smiled at the sound, and he went and opened the narrow door to the hallway.

Through the darkness, his grandfather descended.

A moment later, the man stepped into the light, paused and smiled.

"I can hear you, James," his grandfather said.

"Of course, you can," Jim said, smiling. He stepped aside and the blind man moved easily into the kitchen. With several quick taps of his cane, Jim's grandfather found his chair, pulled it out and sat down.

"Hi, Dad," Jim's mother said, bringing a bowl of mashed potatoes to the table. She set them down and gave him a quick kiss as she brushed his white hair back behind his ears.

"Hello, Karen," he said with a grin. "Carrots, too?"

"Of course," she said, turning to the stovetop.

He turned his head to Jim. "And you, how was school today?"

"About the same as every day," Jim said. He grabbed the salt and pepper, brought them to the table and sat down across from his grandfather.

The man frowned. "Who did you fight today?"

"Dad," Jim's mother said, putting the carrots on the table. "He didn't get in a fight today."

"He did," his grandfather said. "I can smell it on him. What have we said about fighting?"

"Not to," Jim said sulkily.

"Did you?" His mother asked, surprised. She stopped by the sink and looked at him.

"Yes," Jim said.

"Who?"

"Carlton Talbot," he said, taking his napkin off the table and making a big production of spreading it over his lap.

"Why?" she asked.

"Because he's a bully," Jim said, trying not to snap at her. "I don't like it when he pushes me. And I hate it when he pushes other people."

"Who did he push?" his grandfather asked sternly.

"John Petroules," Jim said.

"The crippled boy?" his mother asked as she sat down.

"Yeah," he answered.

"What happened?" his grandfather asked. "What did you do?"

"I punched him," Jim answered. He took a sip of his water and saw that his hand didn't shake.

"Where?" His grandfather said.

"Kidney," Jim replied, and before any other questions could be asked, he said, "no, I didn't get in trouble. Mrs. Couture was out of the room when everything happened."

"Did you get hit?" his mother asked.

"Yeah. Matt Espelin hit me just before the teacher came in," Jim said. "But I don't care. I'll get him tomorrow."

"No," his mother said angrily, "you won't. You know how I feel about fighting."

"Come on, mom," Jim said. "You married dad, he's a soldier. Grandpa was a Marine."

"I am a Marine still," his grandfather snapped. "I also gave my eyes for our country, Jim. Your mother and I don't like you fighting. You know that. Do not get Matt back tomorrow."

Jim opened his mouth to answer, but his words were drowned out by the roar of sirens.

His mother got out of her chair and left the room. She came back a minute later, and said, "A cruiser and a pair of ambulances just pulled in at the Church."

"Do you want me to go see what's going on?" Jim asked eagerly, pushing his chair away from the table.

"No," his mother said, shaking her head. "I'm sure we'll learn soon enough."

"Your mom's right, James," his grandfather said. "Town's too small for information not to rip through it. We'll see how much of it is the truth when all is said and done."

The phone rang, and Jim's mom answered it.

"Hey, Alice. No… no, I don't know what's going on…" his mother said. Her eyes took on a faraway look, and she brushed a stray lock of brown hair back into place. "Oh, well, do they know who… really? Okay. Alright. Yes, yes, thank you, Alice, I'll talk to you soon."

She hung up and looked to Jim before she sat down. Quietly, she interlocked her fingers and set her hands on the table.

Jim's heart beat nervously.

She's upset, he thought. She only did the finger trick when she was really, *really* worried.

"What is it, Karen?" His grandfather asked.

"Alice Wetherbee," Karen said, pronouncing each syllable carefully. "She said two boys are hurt in the Church."

"Who?" Jim asked.

"Carlton Talbot and Matt Espelin," his mother said, looking at him. "James Joshua Bogue, did you have anything to do with this?"

"No," Jim said, surprised at the question.

"I hope not," his mother said in a low voice. "I'm pretty sure the police are going to ask you the same thing."

CHAPTER 4

THE FIRST CONGREGATIONALIST CHURCH

Brian didn't see anyone who was dead.

And he was happy as hell about it.

He was afraid to meet the ghost who had destroyed the eyes of the two teenagers. Brian had seen enough combat related injuries in his time, but the loss of an eye disturbed him. The thought of complete blindness scared him even more than Florence had, and Florence had been terrifying.

Brian leaned against his car and smoked a cigar. He tried to keep calm as he watched the police speak with Reverend Joe. The Rev nodded and then pointed at a tall, saltbox Victorian, which stood on a corner half a block away from the Church.

Brian took his phone out and sent Jenny a quick text.

Hey Babe, can you do a search and see if any type of ghost specializes in blinding people.

He reached into the car, tapped the head of the cigar into the ashtray and turned back to the Church. The Reverend nodded to the police and then walked to Brian as the officers headed towards the Victorian.

"Reverend," Brian said.

"Mr. Roy." He took a handkerchief out of his back pocket, wiped the back of his neck and sighed.

"I'm assuming the injuries are permanent?" Brian asked.

The Rev only nodded.

"But, they'll both live?" Brian said.

"I think the EMTs said so," Reverend Joe said, with a sigh. "There's really no way to tell. I've known people to die of shock from injuries such as those."

"And I've seen men joking with their buddies after losing both legs below the knees," Brian said evenly.

The Rev looked at him, shocked.

"Of course, shock could kill them," Brian said. "My point is, I've seen a hell of a lot worse things happen. I think the boys will be okay. They're young, resilient, and if they have any sort of fight in them, they'll be fine."

"I certainly hope so, Mr. Roy," the Reverend said, looking at the Victorian. "I do certainly hope so."

A stately, elegant woman stepped out the front door of the Church. With long, even strides, she walked directly to Reverend Joseph.

"Reverend," she said, coming to a stop a few feet away.

The woman looked to be in her seventies, but Brian suspected she might be older. Her silver hair was pinned back neatly, and she wore light makeup. Pearls hung from her ears, and while the clothing she wore was aged, it was clean and well cared for.

"Ah, Mrs. Staples," the Rev said, giving the woman a warm smile. "This is Brian Roy."

Brian took the cigar out of his mouth and bowed slightly. "Mrs. Staples. Would you mind if I put the cigar in the car before we speak? I don't want the smoke to bother you."

Mrs. Staples smiled and nodded in approval.

Brian took care of the cigar and turned back to her, saying, "My apologies."

"Not at all, Mr. Roy," she said. "My late husband enjoyed cigars, and he put them away when I was near. I appreciate you doing the same. Before we begin, however, I came out primarily to give this to the Reverend."

She took a cellphone out of her coat pocket and handed it over.

The Reverend nodded. "Thank you."

"Whose is it?" Brian asked.

"One of the boys, we presume," Mrs. Staples said.

"I asked her to hold onto it for me," the Reverend said, blushing slightly. "I didn't want to risk the police seeing me with it."

"Why didn't you give it to the police?" Brian asked, confused.

"Because," the Reverend said uncomfortably, "we're not exactly sure what happened, and I'd rather see if anything is on it. Now, the video selection was on when I found it. I suspect those two were recording something."

"As do I," Mrs. Staples said. "Now, if you will excuse me, I have to go and clean the office, as soon as the police are done in there."

Mrs. Staples looked at Brian and said, "Blood is terribly difficult to clean."

CHAPTER 5

REVIEWING THE FOOTAGE

The office was a crime scene and taped off.

Brian's phone chimed, and he looked at it quickly.

A text from Jenny.

Nothing, Babe. Be safe. Love you.

Love you too, he sent back before he put the phone away.

Brian looked up and nodded at the Rev. The two of them sat in a pew in front of the pulpit. Reverend Joe's hands shook as he passed the boy's cellphone to Brian.

The smart phone was a newer Samsung model, unlocked, and easy to use. When he brought the video up, Brian muted the sound. He was pretty sure the Reverend wouldn't handle any noises well.

Especially since they were probably going to see, if not hear, at least one of the boys being blinded.

"You don't have to watch this," Brian said.

The Rev nodded. "I may not be able to."

"No shame," Brian said. "No shame at all. Are you ready?"

"Yes."

Brian hit play.

A headless figure stood just inside of the room. He wore a uniform, absent of insignia or rank, but it was khaki and looked like it came from World War Two. The dead man's hands opened and closed.

"There's Carlton," Reverend Joe said, pointing at the boy in the shot, who was filming the ghost as well. "This is Matt's phone then."

Brian only nodded. He was more intent on the footage.

The camera remained focused on the headless man, who advanced towards Carlton. The boy, in turn, took a nervous step back.

But not far enough, and not quickly enough.

The ghost brought his hands up and grabbed Carlton's head. The headless man buried his thumbs in the teenager's eyes.

Reverend Joe whimpered and turned away.

Brian didn't.

He watched the boy collapse and the ghost shake the jellied remnants of Carlton's eyes off of his thumbs. The camera stayed on the headless man as he moved towards Matt.

A second later, the screen went dark.

Brian put the phone down on his leg and looked at the Reverend.

"It's alright now, Reverend," Brian said soothingly. "It's over. What I don't understand though, is why didn't the second boy run? Why did he keep recording?"

Cautiously, he turned back to face Brian and avoided the phone. "I really don't know, Brian. But I have to say, I've never seen anything so terrible."

I have, Brian thought. But he kept the information to himself. "It's bad. No doubt about it. Now, put this out of your head. What's done is done, and it's terrible. We need to focus on figuring out why the ghost is here. The uniform is definitely a military one, and I'll look online to see if I can spot it. It looks familiar. Can you start talking to some of your church members and see if anyone has brought anything of a military nature into the building?"

"You think someone did this on purpose?" the Reverend asked, looking horrified at him.

Brian shook his head. "No, not necessarily. Sometimes, things happen. Ghosts cling to objects. If the object was brought here, a donation, anything, the ghost could be stuck here. Do you think you can start asking around?"

"Yes," the Rev answered. "Yes, of course, I can."

"Excellent. Now, can I borrow this phone?" Brian asked. "I'd like to use a still photo of the ghost to try and identify the uniform. Also, I need to listen to it. I want to hear if the ghost said anything."

"How?" the Reverend asked. "He's headless?"

Brian gave him a small smile. "Why not? He shouldn't be here to begin with."

Reverend Joe frowned for a minute, and then he smiled tiredly. "Yes. Yes. You're right."

He stood up and looked down at Brian. "I'll start asking around, Mr. Roy. And I must visit the boys at the hospital. I'll need to check in on their parents as well."

"Could I have your cellphone number?" Brian asked. "Just in case, something comes up?"

"Yes," the Rev said. He took a business card out of his breast pocket and handed it to Brian. "I have your number still."

"Good," Brian said. He put the phone in his pocket as he stood. "I'll give you a call as soon as I find anything out."

"I will do the same, Mr. Roy."

They shook hands and Brian left the church.

He needed to find a place with Wi-Fi so he could do some research.

CHAPTER 6
AN INTERVIEW

Jim wasn't nervous, although his mother looked like she was ready to crawl up the walls. She tapped her fingers on the top of the dining table, which still had the dirty dishes from dinner on it.

His grandfather remained in his seat, his eyelids permanently closed, his hands clasped loosely together on the lap of his black pants.

Jim's mother had put the leftovers into the fridge when the police had knocked on the door.

One was a male state police detective, the other, a female Rye police officer.

They don't look happy, Jim thought.

The Rye cop was a woman. She didn't have any makeup on as far as Jim could see, and her black hair was pulled back into a ponytail. Her dark blue uniform and the body armor under it, hid her shape, so he couldn't tell if she was naturally big, or just a little large from the protective gear. She had thin lips, though, and there was a deadly look of seriousness in her brown eyes.

The detective looked like he should have been a school teacher. He almost had a happy-go-lucky air about him. He didn't look anything like a detective. His hair was a light brown, short, and his face was thick. His eyes were a lighter brown than the Rye officer's, and there were white hairs scattered through the neat beard he wore.

The man's thick fingers idly played with a pen, and occasionally he reached out to adjust the position of a spiral bound notebook in front of him.

"Now," the man said, "my name is Detective Dan Brown, and this is Officer Raelynn French."

Jim's mother nodded. "You can call me Karen. This is my father, Luke

Allen, and my son, James."

Officer French nodded, but Detective Brown grinned and extended his hand to Jim.

"A pleasure to meet you, James," he said. He turned to Jim's grandfather and said, "Is it rude to offer my hand?"

"It'd be rude not to," he replied evenly. He offered his hand, waited for the detective to grasp it, and shook it firmly. "Pleased to meet you, sir."

"Same here. Now, you're not any relation to Luke Allen, who played football for UNH, are you?" Detective Brown asked.

Jim's grandfather grinned. "I'm the one who played."

"Hell," the detective laughed. "My dad used to bring me to all of the university's home games. You were a hell of a running back."

"When I could see," his grandfather agreed, chuckling.

"What happened, if you don't mind?" Detective Brown asked.

"North Vietnamese sniper," Jim's grandfather, said with a shrug. "Went into the Marines as an officer. The Vietnam War kind of did me wrong."

"Well," the detective said, "it's a pleasure to meet you, Mr. Allen. I enjoyed watching you play."

"Thank you."

"Now, Officer French, do you want to lead off here?" Brown asked.

She nodded, fixed her hard eyes on Jim and asked, "Do you know why we're here, James?"

"The fight at school?" Jim offered up.

"Yes," she said. "The fight at school. Do you want to tell us what happened?"

"Sure," Jim said. He told the police the same story he had told his mother and grandfather.

Officer French took out her own notepad and pen, and Jim watched, mildly curious, as the two officers wrote down most of what he said. When he had finished, Officer French looked at him.

"And what about after school?" she asked.

"What about it?" Jim asked in return. "I took the bus home, came upstairs, played a game of chess with my grandfather, read a little bit, and then I helped with the dinner table."

Officer French paused before she said, "Chess?"

Before Jim could answer, his grandfather interjected.

"You doubt I can play, Officer?" he asked.

The woman blushed, cleared her throat and said hastily, "No. Not at all, sir."

"He's really good," Jim said, glancing at his grandfather. "He remembers where every piece is."

"I bet," Detective Brown said with a chuckle. "Now, Mrs. Bogue, can you confirm your son's story?"

"Story?" his mother asked. The nervousness bled out of her voice. "It's not a story, Detective. He was here. Has been here. He doesn't go out without permission. He knows better. What's this about?"

"Mrs. Bogue," Officer French said, "there was an incident with Carlton Talbot and Matt Espelin. They were severely injured this afternoon."

"Over at the Church?" his mother asked. "We saw the ambulances and the cruisers."

"Yes," Detective Brown said, his voice becoming serious. "We have a phone from one of the boys, and they said something about recording what happened to them, but, well, one of our forensics experts managed to trigger the auto-wipe feature on the phone, and we can't see what's on it. Both of the boys are in emergency surgery, and we won't know all of the details until they're done."

"Then why don't you wait until they're out to ask questions?" Jim's mother asked, looking from Detective Brown to Officer French.

"We'd like to get this settled as quickly as possible," Officer French said. "If James can tell us what he did, it will go much easier for him later on."

"What I did?" Jim asked. "What I did?"

"James," his mother said.

"Mom," he said. "Come on. I got home, lost two out of three games of chess, and read some more of *Republic Commando*. Nothing else!"

21

"James," the detective said, a note of severity creeping into his voice. "James, you're the only one who had an issue with those two boys, and you live across from the Church."

"And I didn't do anything!" Jim snapped.

"We will get to the truth," Officer French said. She started to say more, but Jim's mother cut her off.

"I think we're done talking," she said angrily, standing up. "I've been here since James got home. He hasn't gone anywhere. Thank you for being polite, but I really feel it would be best if you both leave now."

The two police officers nodded and gathered their things.

"Detective," Jim's grandfather said as the cops stood up to leave.

"Yes, Mr. Allen?" Detective Brown asked.

"What happened to them? To the two boys?"

"Someone gouged their eyes out, Mr. Allen," Detective Brown said. "They're both blind."

CHAPTER 7
IN THE BASEMENT

Miles Cunningham had a key, although no one knew it.

He'd made a copy, and he kept it close by.

With the key, he opened the side door to the First Church, slipped in and made his way easily through the darkness. The backpack on his shoulders was black, as were his clothes. Even his sneakers were black, the rubber tread silently on the old linoleum of the basement floor.

Miles made his way down to the boiler room. A sharp twist and downward pull popped the old lock out of the door casing.

From his pocket, he took out a small flashlight, the LEDs covered with red cellophane. The red protected his night vision, let him see and didn't give away his presence to any who might pass by.

But at two in the morning, he doubted anyone would pay attention to the Church.

There was nothing to steal, and no one ever vandalized a Protestant Church. They saved their attentions for the Catholics.

Miles stole easily around the giant, ancient heater. Near the new duct work, he removed a cinder block from the wall and shined his light inside.

A yellowed skull sat on a piece of wood. Jawless and toothless. Empty sockets stared at him.

He put his hands together around the flashlight and gave a solemn bow. When he straightened up, he shrugged off his backpack and opened it. He removed a second skull, as barren of jaw and teeth as the first, and placed it beside its companion.

Once more, he bowed, then returned the cinder block to its place. He shined the light on the floor and made certain there was no trace of dirt, nothing to show he had been there.

No evidence of the cinder block's removal from the wall.

Silently, he closed his pack, returned it to its place, and slipped out of the room.

He closed the door behind him and left the Church. He locked the side door behind him and made his way to his car parked nearly a mile away.

Miles had been in the Church for less than two minutes, and all was as planned.

Chapter 8
Luke Allen, August 15, 1955

The Victory over Japan parade had been short and sweet, and Luke could still taste his hot dog. He switched his bottle of Coke from one hand to the next and walked home.

Mr. Boyd sat on his porch, holding a beer and having an electric fan set on a table.

The man looked at Luke and then called out, "Luke!"

Luke stopped and turned to Mr. Boyd. "Yes, sir?"

"How was the parade, boy?" the man asked, his words slightly slurred.

"Fun," Luke answered.

"Did Homer Ferguson march as well?" Mr. Boyd asked with a frown on his face. Luke had heard his own father complain about the way Homer went on about his military service.

For a moment, Luke wanted to lie, but he decided against it. Mr. Boyd would only get angry if he found out otherwise.

"Yes, sir."

Mr. Boyd muttered something Luke couldn't hear and finished his beer. He put the empty bottle down on the porch floor beside the other half a dozen, reached into an ice bucket and pulled out a fresh beer. With a sharp motion, he struck the cap against the arm of the chair, and the small metal disc spun up into the air.

The man caught it easily and set it down beside the electric fan. He looked at Luke and said, "You busy, boy?"

Luke shook his head.

"Come on up, if you don't mind," Mr. Boyd said. "My wife's visiting her sister in Concord, and I'd appreciate the company."

Pa's probably drunk anyway, Luke thought and realized he really didn't want to be home if his father got too angry at the world.

He went up the cement walkway, climbed the stairs and stood a few feet away from Mr. Boyd.

The man smiled. "Take a seat, boy. Take a seat."

Luke sat on the porch across from Mr. Boyd and took a drink of his Coke.

"Did you know I served with your Pa in the Pacific?" Mr. Boyd asked.

Luke shook his head, surprised. "He doesn't talk too much about it."

"Hm," Mr. Boyd said, taking a pull from the bottle. "I understand. Only a few folks I know was in. I ain't like Homer Ferguson. He pulled supply duty in England for the whole war. Talks like he landed at Normandy, went all the way to Berlin and won the damned war himself."

Mr. Boyd snorted, finished the beer and put it down angrily. In silence, he got himself another fresh one from the bucket, opened it the same way as the previous bottle and looked at Luke. "Sorry, boy. Don't mean to snap."

"It's okay," Luke said. *So long as I'm out of arm's reach*, he thought silently.

"You know, when the Japanese surrendered, none of us believed it," Mr. Boyd said after a minute. "We'd been fighting them for so long, we never thought they'd give up. Hell, we were gearing up for the big push into the Japanese home islands. Well, the Marines were. Six divisions to spearhead the invasion. Casualties would have been terrible."

Mr. Boyd reached out, adjusted the fan slightly, and the cool air washed over Luke.

"War's a terrible business, boy," Mr. Boyd said softly. "Terrible business. I don't march because I know. Same with your father. Some can justify what they've done. Some of us, we've come to love it too much."

The two of them drank in silence for a moment, and then Mr. Boyd smiled. "Your father bring home any trophies?"

"From the war?" Luke asked.

Mr. Boyd nodded.

"No," Luke said. "At least, none I know of. I asked him once, years ago,

26

he said the shrapnel in his rear was trophy enough."

Mr. Boyd chuckled. "Well, he has a point there. I brought home some trophies."

"You did?" Luke said.

"Plenty. Plenty. I was a gunnery sergeant by the time we finished, and no one was going to go through my sea bag," Mr. Boyd said with a snort. He finished half of his beer, grinned and asked, "Do you want to see them?"

Luke felt his eyes widen. "Honest?"

"Honest," Mr. Boyd said, chuckling. The man stood up, swayed slightly, and then walked to the front door. "Come on, boy."

Luke stood up and followed him into the house.

The front room was small and well decorated, and it smelled like roses. Doilies were on the furniture and the side tables. Pictures of family stood in neat rows on the mantle and several shelves. A picture of a young Mr. Boyd in a Marine uniform stood off in one corner.

"I think I weighed a hundred and twenty-five pounds soaking wet when I joined the Marines," Mr. Boyd said, shaking his head as they walked out of the room and into a hallway.

He stopped at a closed door, dug a key out of his pocket and unlocked it. Mr. Boyd flicked on the light and stepped into the room.

"Wow," Luke whispered.

The room was lined with bookshelves, but there weren't any books. War trophies and weapons filled the spaces instead.

Luke saw samurai swords and bayonets. Helmets and pistols. Medals, photographs, shell casings, and skulls.

Six skulls looked at him from a glass display case set in the wall across from the door.

The jawbones were gone, as were most of the upper teeth. The skulls were yellowed with age.

"I took those heads," Mr. Boyd said, pausing to take a drink. "I didn't cut them off or anything. Caught some jerk with them. He had snuck up through the lines, almost got himself killed coming back through. Whipped him good, took his trophies away and sent him along to his commanding officer."

"Why'd you keep them?" Luke asked.

"Hm? Oh, well," Mr. Boyd said, scratching the back of his head. "Those Japanese have some curious customs, you know? Everything's got to be burned together or some other stuff. Not really sure. Thought it was a pretty good joke on them, not being able to get to whatever their version of Heaven is. Anyway, now, I keep them to remember what I went through. And besides, I'm not going to throw 'em out. Those boys were doing what they were told. Same as me."

"Like I was saying before, boy," Mr. Boyd said, looking at him. "You do terrible things in war. Terrible. Once you realize you like it, well, you come to respect others who like it, too. And some of those Japanese, well, they liked it. They liked it a lot."

Mr. Boyd looked around the room silently, and Luke did the same.

He felt strange, as though he and Mr. Boyd weren't the only ones there. A cold sensation moved along the back of his neck, and Mr. Boyd smiled.

"Yes," he repeated. "They liked it a lot, boy."

Several small cups rattled on a shelf.

They were tiny, almost like a little girl's play tea set. But they had Japanese flags painted on the sides and what looked to be Japanese writing.

"Yes," Mr. Boyd murmured. "Give me a minute."

He looked at Luke and grinned. "Looks good, doesn't it?"

"Yes sir," Luke said, smiling.

"Now, don't tell anyone about the skulls," Mr. Boyd said seriously. "I don't need any grief from the mayor about them. He was a Four-F, 'physically unfit' to serve in the military. Kind of funny, since Mayor Arel was the star runner in track for the high school. Course it helps when your uncle's the draft board's physician."

"I won't say anything, Mr. Boyd," Luke said.

"Thanks, kid," Mr. Boyd said. He finished his beer. "Come on. I need a fresh drink, and you should get on home."

Luke nodded and stepped into the hall. Mr. Boyd closed up the room, locked the door and then led the way to the porch.

"Thank you, Mr. Boyd," Luke said.

"You're welcome," he replied, grunting as he sat down and got a fresh drink. He looked at him for a moment. "Your pa gets a little rough when he drinks?"

Luke nodded.

"Okay," Mr. Boyd said, popping the cap on his beer. "Know the feeling. Mine was the same way. You ever need to, you come here and see me. Or the missus, if I'm not here."

Luke swallowed dryly and managed to say, "Thank you."

Mr. Boyd smiled, took a drink and then he said, "You're welcome. Now get on. I'll see you soon, I expect."

Luke nodded, waved goodbye, and made his way home to see how drunk his father was.

CHAPTER 9

AT THE HOTEL ROOM

Brian sat down on the chair in his hotel room. He poured himself a healthy shot of whiskey and knocked half of it back before he set up his laptop. Thirty seconds later, he was online, and the hunt was on.

I know I've seen that style of uniform before, Brian thought. Something to do with Clint Eastwood, which made absolutely no sense, but he went with it.

He navigated to Google search and focused on images. Then typed 'Clint Eastwood War' in the search bar and halfway down the page, he found it.

Clint Eastwood's movie about the Japanese on Iwo Jima.

Brian picked up Matt's phone, brought up the image of the ghost and compared his uniform to the uniform of the Japanese general.

Nearly identical.

Thank God for authenticity in films these days, Brian thought.

He leaned back in the chair, finished his glass and poured himself another shot.

It was time to listen to the video, and the idea wasn't particularly appealing. Brian turned the volume up and got ready to stop the action as quickly as it started. He wanted to hear the ghost speak, if at all, and he didn't want to hear the boys being blinded.

With a deep breath, Brian hit play and listened.

An Asian language spilled out of the phone, and just as it ended, Brian stopped the video.

He couldn't tell if it was Japanese or not, but he knew someone who might be able to.

Brian switched Matt's cellphone for his own, brought up Charles Gottesman's number and called him.

The call went to voicemail.

"Charles," he said. "This is Brian Roy. I've got a language question for you. Give me a call back, or shoot me a text. I'm up in Rye on a job."

Brian ended the call, put his phone down and tapped his fingers on the keyboard.

"Now, why," he said into the silence of the room, "is there a headless Japanese ghost in a Protestant church in New Hampshire?

CHAPTER 10

THE REV AND HIS OFFICE

Reverend Joseph Malleus felt extremely uncomfortable in his office.

He had wanted to hire a specialized company to clean the boys' blood up, but Mrs. Staples had refused to let him. She had assured him that she had cleaned worse, and then she set herself to the task.

Although he shouldn't have been surprised at her abilities, he was.

She had removed any trace of the incident.

It was a blessing.

However, he could still visualize the scene. Joe remembered what the two boys looked like in their shared hospital room, the parents who sat in the institutional chairs of blue vinyl and waited for their sons to regain consciousness.

The police waited, too.

They suspected Jim Bogue, which Joe felt, was ridiculous, but he knew the boys would correct the police in regards to Jim.

Still, the question remained, *Where had the ghost come from?*

Why was it there?

And how could a Church be haunted?

It was a place of worship, protected by the light of God.

At thirty-six years of age, Joe had experienced a great many difficulties as the shepherd of his flock. He had guided people through divorces, the deaths of spouses and parents, siblings, and children. Alcoholism and drug abuse, Joe had counseled people and consoled them. He had taught people and brought others into the light of Christ.

How can this place be haunted? he asked himself. Joe knew it was a bit of pride that asked the question, but he didn't feel it was misplaced.

A headless ghost shouldn't be able to haunt a Church.

It definitely should not have been capable of blinding Matt Espelin and Carlton Talbot.

Joe pinched the bridge of his nose and closed his eyes. He tried to focus, tried to understand what was in his Church.

The heating system rattled and grumbled as the furnace kicked in.

A knock sounded on the office door.

The one which led to the hall.

Joe straightened up, opened his mouth to say 'Come in' and then he closed it.

The Church was locked up.

There shouldn't be anyone in the building other than himself.

The door shook with a second knock.

It's not locked, Joe realized.

He glanced at the exit. Slowly he stood up, and the chair's wheels squealed loudly.

The knob turned, and the door swung open.

Nothing stood there.

A voice asked a question in a language Joe couldn't recognize, and one he didn't try figuring out.

He ran for the exit.

Something screamed behind him, and the window to the left shattered. Shards of glass buried themselves in his arm as he reached for the door, but Joe's adrenaline pumped viciously through him.

He ripped the door open and flung himself from the building. His feet caught on the last step, and he smashed face first into the asphalt.

Yet he managed to get up and run.

Off to the right, he saw the kitchen light on in Mrs. Staples' house, and he ran for it.

From the office, the unseen creature shrieked out a question Joe couldn't understand, and with the Lord's Prayer on his mangled lips, he sought refuge with the old woman.

CHAPTER 11
DETECTIVE DAN BROWN TIMES IT RIGHT

Dan had been a cop for twenty years, and he had seen a lot.

Two boys with their eyes gouged out was a new one, though.

He rubbed the back of his neck for a minute and glanced at his watch.

Twenty to one in the morning, he thought. A sigh escaped his lips, and the elevator door opened.

The hospital in Lebanon, New Hampshire was never exactly quiet, but it was strangely peaceful on the ward as he stepped out into the bright fluorescents. Beneath the smell of cleansers, he could smell sickness, and his skin crawled.

Dan hated hospitals ever since he'd watched his mother die of cancer when he was a boy.

With a grunt, he pushed aside the memories of childhood trauma and walked towards Matt Espelin and Carlton Talbot's shared room. The night nurse looked up from her station, and he smiled at her as he came to a stop.

"Detective Dan Brown, New Hampshire State Police," he said in a low voice as he took his badge out. He handed it to her so she could look at it. The young Spanish woman jotted his badge number down in the visitor log along with his name, and smiled as she handed it back.

"How are the boys in one-twelve?" he asked.

"Quiet," she answered, glancing over at the room. "The mothers are in there now."

"How are they?"

The nurse shook her head. "Not good. I think they may have fallen asleep, but they wake up any time we pass by the room."

"Not surprised," Dan said.

A noise came from the room, and he and the nurse looked at the open doorway.

"Hello?" a voice asked. "Hello?"

A boy's voice. Tired and stressed.

The nurse stood up, and Dan followed her into one-twelve.

Mrs. Espelin and Mrs. Talbot blinked as they sat up in their chairs. One of the boys, it looked to be Matt, sat up in his bed. His eyes were bandaged, and he had unshaven blonde stubble on his face. The pale blue hospital johnny, he wore, hung on him.

"Matt," Mrs. Espelin said, panic threatening to burst from her. "Matt, I'm here, baby."

"Mom?" Matt said. "Mom, oh Jesus, Mom is this real?"

His voice climbed an octave.

"Yes," she said, standing up and grabbing his hand. "Yes, but I'm right here."

"Oh no," he moaned, collapsing back against his pillow. "Oh no, no, *no!*"

Carlton continued to sleep.

Dan stepped forward and tapped Mrs. Espelin on the shoulder. Her head snapped around, and when she recognized him, she nodded.

"Matt," Dan said in an even voice, "my name is Detective Dan Brown. I was wondering if you could tell me what happened to you."

The boy bit his bottom lip, and his chin trembled.

"Matt," Dan said softly, "you're not in trouble. I can promise you right now. You are not in trouble, okay?"

"Okay," Matt whispered.

"Good," Dan said. "Very good. Now, tell me what happened, please. I really need to know."

"We heard about the ghost," Matt said in a low, husky voice. "We wanted to see it."

Dan fought the urge to ask about the ghost, but he waited.

"So, we had a key. We had stolen it from Mrs. Staples. She thought Jim Bogue had it, but we took it. We wanted to see the ghost, so we snuck in after the Rev left and Mrs. Staples went home. We were there, and sure enough, the headless ghost came in. It spoke some weird language, and then… oh dear God, then it went after Carlton. It used its thumbs," he sobbed, "and it put out his eyes, and I couldn't move. I couldn't run, and it did the same to me."

Dan shook his head. He licked his lips several times and finally asked, "Matt, are you saying a ghost did this to you and Carlton?"

"Yes," Matt whispered.

Mrs. Espelin started to speak, but Dan gently touched her shoulder and shook his head.

"You're sure it was a ghost?" Dan asked.

"Positive," Matt said, a sob bursting out of his mouth. "Oh Jesus, I'm blind."

"Check the phones," a new voice said.

Dan turned to the other bed.

Carlton Talbot lay on his back with his face to the ceiling.

"Check the phones," Carlton said again. "We were recording everything."

CHAPTER 12

JIM AT THE BURIAL GROUND

Jim's mother thought he was at Anthony's house.

He wasn't though.

He was in the burial ground behind the Church, and he waited. Waited for the ghost to come, the rumors of which had ripped through the kids in the youth group.

With any luck, he'd be able to catch sight of it.

Jim didn't feel bad about Matt or Carlton. He hated both of them. Hated them enough to want to see them dead.

Blind wasn't enough for him. His grandfather was blind, and he managed to do a whole lot more than most people.

Jim didn't want either one of the bullies to be able to do anything more than be dead.

His mother wasn't pleased with the situation, of course. She knew Matt and Carlton bullied him, but there was nothing she could do about it. And she hated it when Jim fought.

He didn't fight for pleasure, though.

Jim fought to win.

And he hated both of them.

In the cold air, Jim settled back against a headstone and pulled his hat down over his ears. The month of April was a pain in New Hampshire. Warm and then cold, dry and then wet. The whole "April's showers bring May's flowers" rhyme he had learned in grammar school was constantly on his mind.

An endless loop of doggerel which made Jim roll his eyes when he repeated it to himself.

But the slight chill would be worth it if he could see a ghost.

He wasn't sure how long he was going to have to wait. The light was on in the office, and the Rev's car was in the parking lot. Jim wasn't sure if ghosts waited until nighttime or what. He was more of a science fiction than a horror reader.

A scream sounded from within the Church and interrupted Jim's thoughts.

A second later, the right window exploded inwards and then the back door was thrown open.

Reverend Joe rushed out, tripped over his own feet and landed face first on the asphalt. Jim heard him whimper and quickly get up.

The Rev didn't run for his car, but instead, raced towards Mrs. Staples' house.

Jim watched him for a minute, and then he turned his attention back to the Church.

A headless man stood in the doorway.

He wore a uniform and in his hand he carried a pistol of some sort.

A second headless, uniformed man joined him and he, too, carried a pistol. They stood in the office, and Jim felt as though they knew he was there.

The first ghost raised his pistol, pointed it at Jim and fired.

Flame leaped from the mouth of the barrel, and the crack of the bullet was loud and abrasive.

A hard, painfully cold sensation punched itself through Jim's shoulder, and he screamed in agony. The pain pulsed through him, and Jim staggered to his feet. It looked as though the ghost would shoot him again, but the other headless man slapped the first one's arm down.

Jim stumbled his way out of the burial ground. His left arm hung uselessly at his side as he ran home.

The pain was intense and churned within his stomach. He slipped, staggered, and fell against a tree for a minute. Vomit exploded out of his mouth, and Jim gagged. He spat the foul remnants of bile out of his mouth before he risked a glance back at the Church.

The doorway was empty.

The ghosts hid within the building once more.

Jim turned towards home and hurried along the sidewalk. Horrific pain thundered through his arm, and he dry heaved, but he didn't stop.

He needed to get to his house.

He needed to be safe.

CHAPTER 13
UNPLEASANT NEWS

Luke Allen knew where everything in his small apartment was.

He had mapped it out decades before, shortly after Robin had left him for a man who was 'whole'. Which was what she had told their daughter, who in turn had refused to leave her father.

Each piece of furniture, and he didn't have much, had been in the same place for the past twenty-five years.

Might be repetition, but it kept him from tripping over the couch.

Luke walked to the stove, found the teapot, reached out, found the tap, and got everything ready for tea.

The house thrummed slightly under his feet. The refrigerator hummed and downstairs, someone came home.

The clock had recently chimed eight.

James is at Anthony's, Luke reminded himself.

He turned around and leaned against the counter. Soon, the water would boil, and there was no need to sit down until it did so.

James' feet sounded on the stairs which led up to Luke's rooms.

A moment later, his grandson knocked on the door.

"Come in, James," he said.

He heard him come in, heard the distress in the boy's respiration.

"What's wrong?" Luke asked.

"My arm," James whispered.

"Tell me," Luke said.

"I… I was shot."

Luke's nostrils flared and instantly sought out the heavy, metallic scent of blood.

Yet, he smelled nothing.

He could hear the boy's fear, the sincerity in his voice.

James wasn't lying.

"Come here," Luke said.

James walked to him.

"Which arm?" Luke asked.

"The left," he answered.

"Get the arm free," Luke said, "and put my hand on the place where it hurts."

He heard the boy whimper for a moment, and then he felt James' small hand take his and guide it to the spot.

Luke gently worked his fingers around the area. Only once did James gasp in pain, and it was when Luke pressed on a spot of flesh which felt as though ice had been applied to it.

"How is it feeling?" Luke asked, taking his hand away.

"It's starting to hurt less," James said, and Luke could hear him putting his shirt back on.

"Tell me exactly what happened, James."

James told him about the burial ground. About the headless ghosts. The shooting.

Headless, Luke thought. A dark fear spread out through him and his guts twisted in a way reminiscent of his time in Vietnam.

"What were they wearing, James?" he asked sternly.

"Uniforms," James answered. "I don't know what type, though. They looked old. They had those weird things wrapped around the bottom of their legs."

"Puttees," Luke said softly. "They're called puttees. What color were the uniforms?"

"Khaki," James said.

"Did you see the gun?" Luke asked.

"Yes," he said.

"Do you remember what it looked like, James?" Luke said.

For a moment, his grandson didn't answer, and then the boy did. "Yes. It looked almost like a German Luger, just not as big."

Luke dropped his head down and rested his chin on his chest.

"What, Grandpa, what is it?" James asked.

"Was Reverend Joseph there? Did he see them?" Luke said instead of answering.

"Yes."

"And was he going towards Mrs. Staples' house?" he asked.

"Yes," James said. "Grandpa, what is it?"

"I'll tell you later, James," Luke said. "For now, I need you to take me to Mrs. Staples' house. We need to speak with the Reverend."

"What do I tell Mom?" James asked.

"Tell her we're going out," Luke replied, turning off the burner beneath his tea kettle. "Just tell her we're going for a walk."

CHAPTER 14

BRIAN DOES SOME RESEARCH

Why are there headless Japanese ghosts in a New Hampshire Protestant church? Brian thought.

That was the real question. If he could answer it, he might be able to figure out a way to stop them.

He also needed to communicate with them, and he needed someone who was familiar with ghosts and who could, at least, understand Japanese.

Which was a pretty narrow niche. Charles Gottesman definitely knew how to handle ghosts, as did his wife Ellen, but Brian didn't know if either of them spoke Japanese.

Brian picked up his cellphone and sent a quick text to Jenny.

Hey Babe, things are quiet. In the hotel right now. Think you could post on the site asking if anyone can speak and understand Japanese?

Jenny's reply came through a minute later. *Japanese? A Japanese ghost?*

Headless Japanese ghost. Blinded two teenagers. Place has never been haunted before. Brian wrote.

Great. Yeah, Babe, I'll post it. Not too much whiskey tonight, okay? You've been giving your heart a run for its money. Leave it be.

Brian nodded. *Yeah. Will do. Love you, Babe.*

Love you, too.

He put the phone down, eyed the whiskey, and decided to wait a little while before the next shot.

With a yawn, he turned his attention back to his laptop, brought up Google again, and started to dig.

Japan, he typed in, *Rye, New Hampshire.*

When he hit enter the page exploded with results.

Long minutes passed as he scrolled through page after page until he found an article.

Brian clicked on it. A newspaper story from nineteen sixty-one.

Local Man, Jonathan Boyd, stops a thief from making off with War Memorabilia, he read. He scrolled down the page, and the rest of the story came into view.

Mr. Jonathan Boyd, a tool and die-maker at the Dartmouth Mill, recently helped to arrest a teenager who had broken into his home.

Mr. Boyd, a decorated Marine, who fought the Japanese, found the sixteen-year-old in his house, while his wife was away in the hospital. The young man, who is known to police for theft and breaking and entering, attempted to get away with some of the items that Mr. Boyd brought home from the war.

Mr. Boyd, who had come home early from work following an electrical malfunction at the Mill, (see yesterday's paper, page 12 concerning transformer issue at Dartmouth), found the young man in the act of stealing.

When Mr. Boyd finally called the police, the young man had to be taken directly to the hospital for treatment. The teenager is currently there, under guard, until he recovers from the injuries sustained while he attempted to flee from Mr. Boyd's residence. This reporter has learned the young man has numerous contusions, one damaged orbital socket, several broken teeth, and three cracked ribs.

His short term memory is also partially impaired.

When we questioned Mr. Boyd about the thief's injuries, his sole response was the young man fell down the stairs.

Several times.

The police served a warrant on the young man's home and found a large amount of property in his bedroom. Anyone who suspects they may have been robbed is encouraged to report to the State Police Barracks 19 here in Rye, and to bring a list of missing items. The police will make every effort to return recovered items to their rightful owners.

Brian shook his head.

War trophies, he thought. It would explain the presence of a ghost in Mr. Boyd's home, but not in the Church. Not unless the dead Japanese soldier was connected to an item present in the Church somewhere.

But it didn't make any sense.

Why now? Brian asked himself.

Before he could think of an answer, his phone rang. A strange New Hampshire number appeared on the screen and then Brian realized it was probably the Reverend.

Brian picked up the phone and answered it.

"Hello?"

"Mr. Roy?" Reverend Joseph asked.

"Right here, Reverend," Brian said. "What's the good word? Did you find anything out?"

"Not really," the Reverend said. "I've had a bit of a bad time. But someone has shown up who might be able to help. Do you think you could meet with us?"

"Sure," Brian said. "When and where?"

"As soon as possible," Reverend Joseph said nervously. "I'm at Eight Washington Street. It's the first left after the Church."

"Okay," Brian said. "I'll be there in a few minutes."

"Thank you," Reverend Joe said. In the background, Brian heard several voices. "Just hurry, Mr. Roy, it's getting worse."

"What do you mean?" Brian asked.

"There are two of them now," the Reverend said.

"Two of who?"

"Two ghosts," Reverend Joe said in a low voice. "Two headless ghosts."

CHAPTER 15

LUKE, MR. BOYD AND SAKÉ, AUGUST 15, 1962

Luke didn't go to the annual parade anymore. Instead, he went to see Mr. Boyd. The year before, Mrs. Boyd had been there, but this year, she was in Concord with her sister again.

He sat at the table with Mr. Boyd. The older man had a beer and Luke had a Coke. Empty plates, which had been graced with hamburgers a short time before, stood on the table.

"The coach from UNH came to talk to me yesterday," Luke said.

Mr. Boyd raised an eyebrow. "What'd he have to say?"

"He wants to make sure I'm going to play football for him," Luke said, grinning.

"Hell," Mr. Boyd said, laughing, "you're only sixteen. Guess you're feeling pretty full of yourself?"

Luke nodded, and Mr. Boyd let out a chuckle.

"Well, leastways you're honest, boy," Mr. Boyd said.

A crash sounded from down the hall, and Luke turned as Mr. Boyd stood up.

The noise had come from Mr. Boyd's war room.

"Luke," Mr. Boyd said in a low voice. "Look at me."

Luke did as he was told. Mr. Boyd's expression was serious, his eyes focused on the door to the war room and not Luke.

"If I say run, you run. Don't ask why. You just go. Understand?"

"Yes sir," Luke replied.

"Follow me," Mr. Boyd said, "and do as I say."

Luke did as he was told and the two of them went to the war room.

Muffled voices slipped out, and Mr. Boyd frowned. He took his key out, unlocked the door and pushed it open.

Luke almost fell down in surprise.

A headless man stood in the room. The image was blurry, though, as if the man was a bad signal on a television set.

But he was real enough, for he turned towards them.

On the floor was a pair of the small china cups decorated with the Japanese flag. A third was in the headless man's hands.

A question was asked in a language Luke didn't understand.

Mr. Boyd replied in the same. Then he turned and looked at Luke. "Go to the kitchen, boy, and set a pan of water on the stove for me. Light the burner and then you best get on home."

"What is it?" Luke asked.

"It is a 'he'," Mr. Boyd said. "And we're thirsty."

"How can he be thirsty?" Luke asked, yet even as the question left his mouth a head appeared on the ghost's severed neck.

A young Japanese man smiled at him and gave Luke a short bow.

"Bow back, Luke," Mr. Boyd said gently. "Ichiru is being polite."

Too surprised not to, Luke bowed.

"Now, on to the kitchen," Mr. Boyd said. "Fix up the water in the pan and get yourself gone. Ichiru and I have some saké to drink."

Numb with confusion, Luke turned away and went to the kitchen to do as he was told.

CHAPTER 16:

A CONVERSATION AT MRS. STAPLES' HOUSE

Mrs. Staples answered the door just a few seconds after Brian rang the doorbell.

"Good evening, Mrs. Staples," Brian said, smiling tightly.

"Good evening, Mr. Roy," she replied, stepping aside. "Please, come in."

Brian did so, and he waited patiently for her to close and lock the door. A faint smell of cat urine permeated the air and a small, orange tabby streaked by. Mrs. Staples led him into her kitchen where he found the Reverend, a teenager and an old man whom he didn't know, at the table.

But Brian was more concerned with the Rev.

The man looked like he'd gone a few rounds with a heavyweight boxer and come out the worse for wear.

"What happened?" Brian asked.

"Sit down," the Reverend said, wincing in pain. "I'll tell you in a moment. First, though, I would like to introduce you to Mr. Luke Allen and his grandson, Jim Bogue."

Brian turned, shook the teenager's hand and then he turned to the grandfather. The man had his hand out, and Brian realized he was blind.

"A pleasure," Brian said, shaking the man's hand.

"Would you care for coffee, Mr. Roy?" Mrs. Staples asked.

"Yes, please," Brian said, sitting down at the table.

"Well," the Reverend Joseph said, clearing his throat nervously. "I had an encounter with the ghosts in the Church."

Mrs. Staples set a mug of coffee in front of Brian. "Cream and sugar?"

"No thank you," Brian said.

She nodded and exited the room.

"There should be six of them," Luke Allen said. The older man's voice was strong and deep.

"Six?" Brian asked, looking at him. "How do you know?"

"I know because I've seen them before," Luke said. He smiled. "I wasn't always blind, Mr. Roy. And because my grandson, here, encountered them right after the Reverend did. He described them to me."

"Do you know why they're in the Church?" Brian asked.

"Yes," Luke said. "They must be looking for their heads."

"So I figured," Brian said. "Why would their heads be in the Church?"

Luke shrugged. "An excellent question. I don't know why they would be. Or how they would have gotten there. They originally were in the possession of a man who had brought them home from the Pacific. He and his wife died in a car accident when I was in Vietnam. I had asked around about his militaria, but no one had seemed to know anything about it."

"And the two ghosts beat you up?" Brian asked, looking at the Reverend.

Reverend Joe shook his head and blushed. "I'm afraid I did this to myself. I panicked and ran, fell down the stairs and landed on my face, unfortunately. I was never particularly graceful."

"I saw it," Jim said, speaking for the first time. His voice cracked slightly and reminded Brian of his own horrible passage through puberty.

"You saw me?" the Reverend asked in surprise.

Jim nodded. "I was hiding in the burial ground. I wanted to see the ghosts."

"Did you?" Brian asked.

"Yes," Jim replied. "And they saw me or noticed me. Whichever it is. One of them shot me."

Brian looked at the boy in surprise. "Shot you? How?"

The boy shrugged, winced and then he said, "I'm not sure. He pointed a pistol at me, pulled the trigger, and it went off. I felt something hit my shoulder. It feels better now, but it was really bad at first."

"The place where there should have been a wound was cold," Luke added.

"Great," Brian murmured. He played with the iron ring on his right hand nervously. "Okay. Let me see if I've got all of this straight. First, we had one headless ghost who came along and blinded a couple of teenagers. Second, another headless ghost showed up. So now, we have two. Third, Luke here, knows about them, and he's pretty sure they're looking for their heads. Fourth, they can shoot phantom bullets."

Brian sighed and looked around at the others. "Anything I forgot?"

"Yes," Luke said. "The heads are somewhere in the Church, and there are four more we have to worry about."

"Great," Brian said, shaking his head. He picked up his coffee, drank a little of it and looked at Luke. "Well, Luke, evidently these ghosts have been around for a while. Have they killed before?"

"No," Luke answered.

"Do you know why?"

Luke shook his head. "No. The only man who did know was Jonathan Boyd, and he's been dead for over forty years."

Brian frowned, rubbed the back of his head and said, "Where's he buried, Luke?"

"What?" Luke asked, confused.

"Do you know where he's buried?" Brian asked again.

"No," Luke said. "I'm sure we can find out, though."

"Good. Let's make locating Mr. Boyd's final resting place our top priority," Brian said.

"Why?" Jim asked.

"I want to see if he's still hanging around," Brian answered. He drank his coffee, and then he smiled. "If he is, I'll ask him what it was he did to keep them happy."

"What?" The Reverend asked. "What do you mean, 'ask him'?"

"I can see the dead, Reverend," Brian said, his smile fading. "And I can talk with them, too."

CHAPTER 17

A TALK

Jim sat in his grandfather's sparse apartment and sipped his tea. It was after ten thirty and his mother hadn't been happy about him being out so late.

His grandfather didn't tell her about Jim's little trip to the burial ground. Or their walk over to Mrs. Staples' house.

Jim thought about the man, Brian Roy. He seemed to be focused, and determined. Not too tall, not too thin, but bald, bearded and he looked like he had killed more than a few people. The man's matter-of-fact desire to speak with the dead, as well as his supposed ability to do so, was unnerving.

Jim's sole run-in with the headless ghosts had been enough. He didn't want to meet any more.

"James," his grandfather said.

"Yes?" he answered.

"Worrying about the dead?"

"Yes."

"Don't," his grandfather said. "Worry about problems you can control. The dead aren't one of those."

"Do we have to go with Mr. Roy?" Jim asked.

His grandfather nodded and then he carefully brought his tea up to his mouth.

"Why?"

"Because I knew Mr. Boyd, James. I knew him well," his grandfather said. "He helped instill in me a desire to serve our country, just like he had. We all have to sacrifice, although service isn't a popular theme in today's society."

Jim knew his grandfather needed him, especially in an unfamiliar place.

Still, after the whole incident in the burial ground, Jim wasn't thrilled with the idea of going near any more cemeteries.

"I know," Jim said finally. "I just don't want to see any more ghosts."

His grandfather nodded. "Yes. I understand. I didn't want to see any ghosts either, but I did."

"You really saw them?" Jim asked. He didn't exactly doubt his grandfather, but he still found it hard to believe. Even after what he had experienced.

"Yes," his grandfather said. He finished his tea, set the cup down on the table effortlessly, and turned his closed eyes towards Jim. "Yes, I saw them. I have few visual memories anymore, James. The ghosts, though, the ghosts I remember. I remember them well."

"How many times did you see them?" Jim asked in a low voice, as though the headless men could hear him.

"Three times," his grandfather answered. "Three times more than necessary, as far as I'm concerned. But you really can't take back what you've experienced."

"Yeah," Jim agreed. He drank the last of his tea and put the cup beside his grandfather's. "Do you know when we'll go?"

"As soon as we find out where Mr. Boyd is buried."

"Even if it's dark?" Jim asked.

His grandfather smiled. "A little courage, James. It's always dark for me."

CHAPTER 18

THE PHONE CALL

The phone rang and woke Brian up.

He blinked, looked around and realized he had fallen asleep in the chair. It took him a moment to recognize the unfamiliar hotel room and pick his phone up off the table.

"Hello?"

"Brian, it's Charles Gottesman."

Sleep fled Brian's brain, and he straightened up. "Charles, thanks so much for getting back to me."

"No worries," Charles said. "Sorry, it took me so long to call you. Ellen and I were out in Pennsylvania the past couple of days. Native American war club."

"Damn," Brian said, impressed. "Difficult?"

"Extremely," Charles said, chuckling. "Had a hard time finding someone we could bribe to get into the museum where it was being kept. Anyway, what's going on?"

"I'm working a job up in Rye," Brian said. "I've got a headless ghost. Japanese soldier. I was wondering if you or Ellen spoke Japanese."

Charles laughed. "No, Brian, I'm sorry."

Brian groaned. "Damn. I don't want to bring anyone outside of the ghost hunting community in on this."

"Understood," Charles said. There was a slight pause and then he said, "I may know someone. He's got a knack for languages."

"Is he okay with the dead?" Brian asked seriously.

"Yes," Charles answered. "More than okay. If you like, I can pass on your info to him. Let him decide if he's interested. He's a private guy."

"Fine with me, Charles," Brian said. "I can pay him if he needs it."

"I'll let him know. I'll give him your phone and email address," Charles said.

"Great," Brian said, sighing with relief. "Can you ask him to call, rather than email? I think this case is going to be a tough one, and I may be a little too distracted to check my account."

"Got it. Say hi to Jenny for us," Charles said.

"And to Ellen for us, Charles. Talk to you soon."

Brian ended the call and returned the phone to the table. With a grunt, he stood up, his knees popped, and his back ached. He splashed a little whiskey into the tumbler, knocked it back and then made his way to the bathroom.

He needed some comfortable sleep.

Tomorrow, he would have to speak with the dead.

CHAPTER 19

OFFICER RAELYNN FRENCH INVESTIGATES

Raelynn had gotten a call from Dan the day before, and she hadn't believed it.

The two blind teenagers had told him it was a ghost who had hurt them.

A ghost, she thought, disgusted.

She parked her cruiser on the street in front of the First Congregationalist Church.

It was seven in the morning.

She called in her position and turned the engine off. After she got out, she adjusted her vest and made her way towards the back of the building. Dan had told her both the boys recorded the incident. The problem she and Dan had, however, was the presence of only one phone.

One wiped phone because an overeager tech had accidentally triggered a safety feature.

More than likely both boys had been recording. Which meant there should have been two phones, but one was missing.

Logic, therefore, dictated the other was somewhere in the office.

Reverend Joseph Malleus was a man who got to work early. Or at least, people had said he did.

His car wasn't there, however.

Raelynn continued around the back and stopped sharply.

The back door was open, and the window to the right of it was shattered, broken inwards.

She reached up to her shoulder and keyed the mic which hung from her epaulet.

"Base, this is Three-Three," Raelynn said. "I have a possible break-in at the First Church."

The sound of breaking dishes cut her off.

"Three-Three going in!" she said, dropping her hand from her shoulder to her sidearm. With an easy, long practiced motion she drew the semi-automatic and hurried up the steps.

"Rye Police!" she yelled, and entered the building.

The door from the office to the rest of the Church was open, and Raelynn stepped up to it. She paused, looked quickly out into the hall and saw nothing. She waited and was rewarded with the sound of something being smashed a few doors up to the right.

With her weapon ready, Raelynn moved forward. Another crash sounded, and she saw that the third door was slightly open.

She kicked the door open, braced herself for a confrontation and called out, "Rye police, hands up!"

Raelynn froze.

Two headless men stood in front of her in a small kitchen.

Glasses were broken on the floor and silver plated serving trays were scattered across a long, stainless steel counter. Water ran steadily from the faucet. A large, industrial refrigerator stood open and its bright light shined partially through the two ghosts.

Raelynn blinked, unsure of what to do.

The dead men didn't hesitate. They drew curious pistols from holsters at their sides, and they fired.

The simultaneous shots deafened her even as the bullets punched through her flesh. Somehow, the rounds passed through her vest, and she felt them slam into her heart. As she fell backward from the force of the blows, her trigger finger squeezed reflexively. She fired off a single shot, which buried itself in the far wall.

Raelynn landed on the floor with a thud and her breath exploded out of her as she felt her heart stop.

It was a strange, worrisome sensation.

I'm dying, she thought. Her eyes closed and she couldn't catch her breath.

The sounds of the world became muffled, and she shuddered.

Why won't my heart start up? she asked herself, darkness sweeping over her. *Why?*

Why won't it start?

Raelynn gasped for air, and couldn't think of anything other than her mutinous heart.

CHAPTER 20
LOOKING FOR MR. BOYD

The morning was cold.

The sun hid behind a bank of dark clouds, and Brian felt certain there'd be rain, regardless of the forecast.

He leaned against his car, smoked the last of his cigar, and saw Reverend Joe. The Rev was in the lead with Luke and Jim a few steps behind. Luke used a white, red-tipped cane with ease while he kept his free hand on Jim's shoulder. The teen looked completely comfortable with his grandfather, and for a moment, Brian wondered if his own grandfather lurked around his grave.

Brian had loved the man dearly.

He pushed the thought away and looked, instead, at the Central Cemetery in Rye. Inside, among all the other graves, they would find Mr. Jonathan Boyd's. At first glance, it seemed as though the job would be an easy one.

But in the corners of his eyes, Brian caught movement. The shadowy and hazy movement of the dead.

There were plenty of people buried in Central who either didn't know they were dead or just didn't care. Brian wasn't looking forward to it.

Not at all.

"Good morning," he said around the stump of his cigar.

The Reverend smiled and then winced.

Brian wasn't surprised. The Rev's face looked worse than it had, the night before.

"Good morning indeed," Luke said.

They stopped beside Brian.

"Do we know where he is exactly?" Brian asked.

"Yes," the Reverend said. "Lot Q, row seven, grave four."

"Okay," Brian said, looking through the gates. "Got an idea as to where Q is?"

"Up and to the left," Reverend Joe said.

Brian looked and repressed a shudder.

He saw, at least three dead men, and one very old dead woman on the way there.

And they looked at him.

Brian sighed.

"Something wrong, Mr. Roy?" Luke asked.

"Wrong? No. Discouraging? Yes," Brian replied.

"What's going on?" Jim asked, looking out into the cemetery, but obviously not seeing what Brian did.

"The dead, Jim," Brian said, and he had to fight the urge to imitate Dr. McCoy. "There are a few I can see. They know I can see them. I'm just hoping they won't do anything."

Jim nodded his agreement.

"So, Luke," Brian said. "You knew Mr. Boyd?"

"I did," Luke answered.

"Good man?" Brian asked.

"The best," Luke said soberly.

"Good," Brian said. "Should make it a little easier to talk to him, then, if he's still there."

With a deep breath, Brian tucked the cigar in between the side mirror and the door frame, squared his shoulders and led the way into the cemetery.

He kept a steady pace and glanced back only once to make sure Luke was able to keep up.

The man did so, easily. The cane tapped on the cracked asphalt of the cemetery road and Jim lent his support. Reverend Joe walked behind them.

With each ghost they passed, Brian could feel their undead eyes upon him. He could sense the unasked questions, the desire to know who he was and why he was there.

Soon, they were near the back of the cemetery, and the Rev said, "Turn left here. This is lot Q."

Brian did so.

He found the right row, and then the proper grave.

"Jonathan Daniel Boyd," Brian read aloud. "Born September 4, 1917. Died January 4, 1968. Gunnery Sergeant, United States Marine Corps. Purple Heart, Bronze Star, Silver Star, Navy Cross."

Brian shook his head. "Man was tough."

"He was indeed," Luke agreed.

"Is he here?" Reverend Joe asked, looking around. He seemed uncomfortable. It was as though the idea of the dead being anywhere other than Heaven was extremely upsetting.

"I don't know," Brian said, looking around. And then he stopped.

A ghost stood off to one side. He wore a Marine Corps uniform, and he looked to be about fifty years old. The dead man looked steadily at Brian.

"You can see me," the ghost said.

"I can," Brian answered.

"You're looking for someone," the dead man continued.

"I am," Brian agreed.

"Who?"

"Jonathan Boyd," Brian said.

The ghost's eyes widened slightly. "Well, you found him, boy. What do you want with me?"

"We need help," Brian said.

Jonathan Boyd looked at the others, who gazed intently at Brian, yet said nothing. Then Boyd asked, "Who are they?"

"The one with the collar is Reverend Joe Malleus," Brian said. "He's the Reverend over at the First Congregationalist Church. The teenager, his name's Jim Bogue. His grandfather, there, well, you know him. He's Luke Allen."

Jonathan looked at Luke, took a step closer and asked in a low voice, "Why's he blind?"

"Luke," Brian said.

"Yes?" Luke answered.

"Mr. Boyd would like to know why you're blind," Brian said.

The dead Marine shimmered slightly, and from the simultaneous gasp from the Reverend and Jim, Brian knew the ghost had made himself visible.

"Hello, boy," Jonathan said. "You're not a boy anymore."

"No," Luke said, smiling, "I'm not, sir."

"Still polite, though," Jonathan said, nodding. "So, rather than have a go-between, you want to tell me what happened to your eyes?"

"Mr. Boyd," Luke said. "Enemy sniper. The bullet passed clean through one eye and out the other. One of the neatest shots the doctors had ever seen. They had to rebuild my nose, though."

Jim looked at his grandfather with surprise.

Jonathan nodded. "I'm sorry to hear it, Luke. I'm glad you're not dead. You've enjoyed life?"

"I have," Luke said.

"Good, boy, good," Jonathan said. "Now listen, we'll see each other again, and I mean see. You get everything back when you go. We'll swap war stories then, and you can tell me whether you came to love it or not."

"I look forward to it, sir," Luke replied in a low voice.

"Me, too, Luke. Me, too." Jonathan turned his attention back to Brian. "You need my help?"

"Yes, sir," Brian said. "We've got a couple of headless Japanese soldiers who are pretty upset."

"Just two of them?" Jonathan asked with a chuckle. "Usually, all six get worked up at the same time. Well, the best thing to do is get them some saké and heat it up. And why are they headless? Last thing those boys like to do is go around without their heads."

"We were hoping you could tell us," Brian said. "See, we don't know where the heads are."

"They're in my war room," Jonathan said, frowning. "All of the skulls are."

"Sir, your war room was cleaned out when you died. No one knows anything about the skulls," Brian said. "In fact, up until a couple of days ago, the headless men haven't even made a noise."

"It means someone's moved them around," Jonathan said, a mask of anger dropping onto his face. "Someone's been playing with their skulls. Find the skulls, get some saké out, and you'll be able to quiet the boys down. Best to do it quick, too. They get real angry, real easy."

"How do we find the skulls?" Brian asked.

Jonathan looked at him for a moment, as though he were the stupidest person the dead man had ever met. And at the end of the stare, Brian felt exactly like he was.

"You've got to look, boy," Jonathan said. "You've got to look. And make it quick. The longer they wait, the angrier they'll be. And when they get angry, well, they get mean."

"Yeah," Brian said softly, sighing. "Yeah. We figured the last part out."

CHAPTER 21

FORCED TO WAIT

Miles had seen the Reverend leave home much earlier than usual, and he knew he had an opportunity to get into the Church again.

Within a few minutes, he had removed the third skull from the cabinet, packed it up, and made his way out the door. He walked steadily towards the Church. He kept his head up and his gaze focused on the horizon.

He looked like someone hurrying to the bus stop to get to work.

The weight in his pack reminded him he wasn't.

Miles had his work now. Special work. Work which needed to be done.

It took him ten minutes to reach his car. He waited another three minutes to make sure he hadn't been followed, and then he got into his car and made his way to the Church.

He needed to do a drive by to make sure everything was safe.

It wasn't.

There were police officers everywhere, and they directed traffic away from the Church.

Something had happened. Something bad. And Miles knew it.

At the first intersection he came to, he turned his car back towards its parking spot.

He had to get home and get the skull back into its cabinet before Sato awoke.

Sato didn't like to be awoken.

It was never good to be around when Sato was awake. *Never.*

CHAPTER 22

IN THE RIVERWALK CAFÉ

"I'm sorry," the Reverend said. "But should Jim really be here?"

Before Brian could answer, Luke Allen spoke up.

"Reverend," he said politely. "He has just as much a right to be here as we do."

Reverend Joe cleared his throat nervously. "I apologize, Mr. Allen, I meant, is he old enough? Not if he has a right to be here."

"He's old enough," Brian said. He motioned for the waitress, Lisa, and the young woman came over. Out of the corner of his eye, he saw Jim blush and look down at the table.

"Hi Jim," she said brightly.

The teen's eyes widened slightly as he straightened up and looked at her. "Hi, Lisa."

"Are you drinking coffee now?" she asked.

"Yes," Jim said. "Yes, I am."

"Cool," she said, giving him a wink. "How do you like it?"

"Black," he answered.

She looked at him and smiled. "Wow! I'm impressed. Most of the guys, who come in here, order iced coffees or add so much sugar and cream you can't even recognize the coffee anymore."

Lisa turned her attention to the Reverend. "Hey Rev, spiced tea?"

"Please, Lisa," Reverend Joe answered.

"And for you?" she asked, looking at Brian.

"Black coffee," Brian said.

"I'll have the same, young lady," Allen said, smiling in her direction. The old man had his hands folded together on the table.

"Three blacks and one spiced," Lisa said, nodding her head. "Be back in a couple of minutes, gentlemen."

Jim watched her walk away.

"Is she as pretty as she sounds?" Luke asked Jim.

The young man blushed furiously. "Yes, grandpa."

"Older than you," Luke added.

"Yes," Jim said, sighing.

"Not by much, I'd wager," Luke said. "Give it a year or two, James. You two will be good for each other."

The three of them looked at Luke curiously, and the old man must have felt it. He grinned and said, "Some things, you just know."

They stayed quiet for the few minutes it took for Lisa to get back with the drinks, but once she did, Reverend Joe spoke.

"The skulls are in the Church," he said, repeating what the ghost of Jonathan Boyd had told them. "We need to find them."

"Not only find them," Brian said, "but we need to get saké as well."

"Where are we going to get saké?" Luke asked.

Before Brian could answer, Jim asked a question, "What's saké?"

"Japanese rice liquor," Brian said. "And I know where to get it. Most of the liquor stores carry it, but if they don't, there's a store down in Nashua which usually has a couple of different styles in stock. So, the saké problem is simply a logistics issue. The real concern I have is the church, the size of it. There are a lot of places where things can be hidden, or so I figure."

The Reverend nodded. "Lots and lots of places. The challenge, unfortunately, is seeing if we can find them before the ghosts attack someone else."

"Do you think," Luke said, "we might be able to intercept them?"

"How so?" Brian asked.

"What if one of us, say myself, were to remain in the Church while we sought out the skulls and picked up the saké?" Luke asked.

"The only issue I see with your idea," Brian said, "is, unless I'm wrong here, you don't speak Japanese?"

65

"No," Luke said with a frown. "I'd forgotten about the language barrier."

"Well," Brian said. "I've asked around about Japanese speakers who aren't afraid of ghosts, and I may have found someone. I'm hopeful the person will call."

"Could we close off the Church?" Jim asked in a low voice.

Brian looked at him, as did the Reverend.

"What do you mean, James?" Luke asked.

"The ghosts attack people in or near the Church, right?" Jim asked.

The men nodded in unison.

"So, if that's the case," he continued, "why not close it down? Couldn't we pretend there's an issue with the Church and we can't let anyone in?"

"You've got a good head on your shoulders," Brian said, nodding in appreciation. "What about it, Rev?"

"Hm," the Reverend said, rubbing his chin. "We have a couple of meetings scheduled, but obviously, nothing we can't shunt aside to someone's house. We could say there's an issue with the heating system. No one likes to be cold, especially at the end of winter. Yes. Yes, I think Jim's plan has merit."

Jim smiled. Luke reached out, found Jim's hand and gave it a squeeze.

"Let's get the ball rolling on the failed heating system, then," Brian said. "And let's not discuss this with anyone else. As soon as I get a call back from the man who speaks Japanese, I'll need to get into the church, Reverend."

Reverend Joe nodded. "Not an issue, Mr. Roy."

"Luke, do you think you and Jim could start digging into Mr. Boyd's past? Specifically, around the time he died?" Brian asked.

"What in particular are you looking for?" Luke asked.

"Anything, really," Brian said. "I'm wondering why the ghosts have appeared now when they've been quiet for fifty years?"

"James and I will see what we can find," Luke said.

"We'll figure it out, Mr. Roy," Jim said.

"Please," Brian said, "all of you can call me 'Brian.' Let's finish our drinks and get this solved as quickly as we can. I don't think I'm alone in saying this is a dangerous situation. And we shouldn't let it get any worse than this."

With the last word out of his mouth, the Reverend's phone rang.

Reverend Joe had a look of confusion on his face as he took the cell out of his pocket.

"Hello?" he asked, answering the call.

For several minutes, he listened. Finally, he said, "Yes, yes. Yes, I understand."

He ended the call and put the phone away. The Reverend licked his lips and then looked at them, his expression one of concern.

"Who was it?" Luke asked.

"Detective Dan Brown of the New Hampshire State Police," Reverend Joe said. "He said there's a dead police officer in the Church."

"What?" Brian asked.

"Yes," the Reverend said. "She died of a heart attack. But they don't know why. She was investigating a break-in. And… she died."

All of them were silent for a few moments until Reverend Joe broke it.

"Do you think, Mr. Brian, do you think they killed her?" he whispered.

Brian lifted up his mug, finished his coffee and set it back down again. He looked at the empty porcelain and nodded. "Yes, I do."

CHAPTER 23

IN THE CHURCH

Detective Dan Brown stood in the First Congregationalist Church's kitchen and frowned.

He could smell cordite.

Actual cordite. Not gunpowder. Not propellant. Actual, honest to God *cordite*.

Raelynn hadn't been shot, though.

It looked, as far as the EMTs and the medical examiner could tell, like she had suffered a heart attack.

Twenty-five years old, Dan thought, *and she dies of a heart attack*.

He looked around the kitchen and scratched the back of his head.

The place was a wreck.

Pots and pans and broken glass. Cutlery and plates. White filters and finely ground coffee. Pepperidge Farms sugar cookies and saltine crackers. Someone had ripped through the kitchen and its cabinets. But there wasn't a trace of anyone.

No footprints, no trace of evidence, not a single thing to show an actual person had been in the kitchen when Raelynn had come into the room.

A ghost, Dan thought, remembering what Carlton had said.

He scoffed and one of the forensic techs looked over at him.

Dan shook his head, and the techs went back to their evidence collection.

What evidence? he asked himself.

All he had was a dead colleague and one hell of a mess.

Keene dispatch had said Raelynn called in a break-in. Afterward, she had told them she was entering the building.

But why?

Dan looked around.

The destruction of the room definitely indicated someone had been in there. The lack of evidence said otherwise. It was as though a hurricane had started up in the kitchen, ripped it apart, and then vanished.

Not before killing Raelynn though, he reminded himself. Dan turned and looked out the door to where they had found her body.

A perfectly fit young woman, dead of cardiac failure.

An autopsy would be performed. She would be tested for drugs, everything from recreational blends to performance enhancers. They would check with her fiancé and ask to go through the medicine cabinet.

Dan didn't think they would find anything.

A ghost.

The idea wasn't as funny or strange as when he'd heard Carlton talk about it.

Dan wouldn't know for certain until they found the phone which had been misplaced.

For a moment, he thought about the boy, Jim Bogue, and the boy's grandfather.

Then Dan shook his head.

Neither of them would have had anything to do with it.

Just you being stubborn, wanting to cram a round peg into a square hole, Dan chided himself. The evidence didn't point to Jim Bogue, and Dan wasn't about to make it.

He rubbed the back of his head again, caught himself and lowered his hand.

A bad habit he wanted to break.

With a sigh, Dan left the kitchen, walked out to the Church office and took another look.

The room was nearly as wrecked as the kitchen. Someone had tossed it, and not skillfully. This wasn't a professional searching for the money box. It didn't even look like a couple of kids who wanted to create some havoc.

Same as with the kitchen, Dan realized. *Someone is hunting for something. What though?*

The drawers of Reverend Joseph's desk were emptied out. The filing cabinet's items were scattered. The window had been broken in and shattered glass peppered the floor. The door hung by a hinge.

Traces of blood and skin had been found at the bottom of the outside steps on the pavement.

Someone fell, trying to get out.

Someone ran, Dan thought.

Who? Not the one who broke in. No. Someone was scared, he thought, stepping up to the open doorway. *Someone was terrified.*

Who would have been in the office?

Dan smiled. *Why, the Reverend, of course. It's his office.*

He looked up, and a bit of movement caught his eye.

Off to the right, an old woman stood in the side window of her house.

She stepped away, but not before Dan recognized her.

The woman who cleaned the Church. Mrs. Staples.

And who knows everything about a Church? He asked himself. *Well, I'm sure Mrs. Staples would know. Yes, she would.*

Dan put his hands in his pockets, exited the Church and made his way to the front of the old woman's house.

Maybe she could tell him about ghosts.

CHAPTER 24

WAITING

Miles Cunningham left the liquor store with the brown paper bag held tightly to his chest.

It was nearly eight o'clock.

He had barely made it. The clerks in the store had given him the evil eye. He couldn't explain, though, or tell them why it was so important. They had seen him before, of course, but never upset.

They would remember him, and he didn't want them to.

Too late now, he told himself.

Miles walked down the street, turned right and quickly reached his car.

He never parked near the store. He didn't want anyone to see what type of car he drove. Or know his license plate number.

Cautiously, he set the bag on the floor, buckled himself in and started the engine. He needed to get home. They were already upset as it was. Any more of a delay and he might suffer repercussions.

Terrible ones.

He shuddered at the thought of it.

It took him nearly half an hour to get home. He drove the speed limit and made sure to signal where appropriate. Unnecessary attention from law enforcement needed to be avoided.

They always asked too many questions.

When Miles finally turned into his driveway and put the car into 'park', he let out a long, heartfelt sigh of relief. Before he turned off the engine, he looked at the small New England cape which he called home, and he smiled.

With the recent warm spell, he had been able to cut back the huge rhododendron which had hidden most of the first floor. The dull white siding needed a fresh coat of paint, but he would take care of the exterior in the late spring.

He smiled to himself, took the key out of the ignition and carefully picked up the package from the floor. Quickly, he made his way to the side door, unlocked it and slipped into the kitchen.

He turned on the light and glanced down at the bare subfloor.

I still need to tile this, he thought, walking to the counter by the sink. He put the bag down and removed four bottles of saké from it. From the cabinet, he took the tokkuri, opened a bottle of saké and poured the liquor into it. He then removed five of the small sakazuki, the cups delicate and fragile in his hands. Quickly and quietly, he arranged them on the counter. He took the tokkuri, put it into the microwave and set it to forty seconds.

And then Miles heard them.

Their voices rose up angrily from the basement, their footsteps heavy on the stairs.

The microwave hummed, the numbers counted down.

The new, white door opened, and they came up.

He breathed a sigh of relief.

They have their heads, he thought as the microwave beeped loudly and announced it was done.

He bowed low before the four dead Japanese soldiers.

Once he straightened up, Ichiru looked at him and asked, *"Do you have it?"*

"Yes," Miles answered, glancing at the microwave. *"And it is warm as well, sir."*

Ichiru looked at him for a moment.

Does he suspect? he thought nervously. *Does he know what I'm doing?*

"Serve it," Ichiru said, and the dead gathered around the only living man in the house.

With shaking hands, he took the tokkuri out of the microwave, poured the saké into each cup, and offered it to the ghosts.

And they accepted.

CHAPTER 25

A PHONE CALL

Brian picked up his phone and sent Jenny a text.

Two boys blinded. Another boy injured. Cop killed.

She wrote back a moment later.

Sweet Jesus, Babe! Do you think maybe you better pass this one off to someone else?

Brian thought about it for a moment, pictured his one-time assistant and shook her out of his mind.

No, he wrote back, *I can't do that. I'm already here, and the situation needs to be resolved. I only wanted to let you know what's going on.*

Thanks. Be CAREFUL. You know how bad your heart is, and if you become a ghost, I swear I will have you bound to a tiara and put in a preschool.

Brian laughed out loud and shook his head.

I love you, he wrote. *I will be careful.*

Love you, too, Babe, she replied.

With a sigh, Brian put the phone on his lap and leaned back. He closed his eyes and smiled as he thought about Jenny.

Ah, he thought, *to be home, in my chair, with a Booker's neat.*

Then he remembered Leo. Brian pictured the strange little man and the gift he had given him.

No, Brian told himself, *home will have to wait. These people need help. I need to figure out what's going on.*

The phone rang, and Brian nearly jumped out of his seat.

He shook off the surprise, picked up the cell and looked at it.

Unknown caller.

Brian frowned and answered the call.

"Hello?" he asked.

"Hello, is this Brian Roy?" a man asked.

"This is," Brian answered.

"Brian, my name is Shane Ryan. I'm a friend of Charles Gottesman," he said. "Charles told me you have a language problem with a ghost?"

Brian nodded and said, "Yes I do. Well, two now, actually. They're both Japanese soldiers."

"Aggressive?" Shane asked.

"Extremely," Brian said. "I know for certain they blinded two boys, shot, somehow, a third, and we're pretty sure they killed a police officer, too."

"Damn," Shane said. "You're up in Rye?"

"Yes," Brian replied. "So, you speak Japanese?"

"I do," he answered. "Where's a good place to meet?"

"There's a coffee shop on Main Street called the Riverwalk. How long will you be?" Brian asked.

"Give me an hour and a half. I've got to square away some stuff and then I'll grab a car. Riverwalk, you said?"

"Yes," Brian answered. "Listen, I really appreciate this, Shane."

Shane laughed. "No worries. I'll see you at the Riverwalk."

"Okay," Brian said, and he ended the call.

His stomach rumbled and reminded him he hadn't eaten in a long time. With a grunt, he got up from the chair, went to his overnight bag and pulled out his much battered and beloved copy of Max Brooks' *World War Z*.

Brian looked down at the orange cover and smiled.

Thank God I don't have to deal with zombies.

He tucked the book under his arm, grabbed his wallet and keys, and then made his way out of the room.

It was time to see what sort of food the Riverwalk offered.

CHAPTER 26

SEARCHING FOR ANSWERS

Jim sat in front of a computer at the Rye Public Library. His grandfather sat in a chair beside him, and together they sought out information about the dead Japanese soldiers.

Although Jim couldn't figure out how they might do it.

"Now, Jim," his grandfather said, "you'll have to explain to me how this is going to help us."

"Okay, Grandpa," Jim said. "I have what's called a search engine. We'll type in a piece of information, and then it will bring up all sorts of stories and articles related to the stuff we put in."

His grandfather frowned, but nodded a moment later.

"Alright, let's start with something simple. Please type in 'Jonathan Boyd'," he said.

"I'm also going to add 'Rye, New Hampshire,'" Jim said. "The more information we put in, the better."

His grandfather nodded and Jim typed in the name and town and city.

When Jim hit return, the screen shifted, and the various results appeared.

"What does it say?" his grandfather asked.

"Hm," Jim said, leaning close to the screen, "some of them say what we saw on his headstone. But there's one here, it says he caught a burglar?"

"Can you read it to me?"

"Hold on," Jim said. He clicked on the article and waited for it to load. Once it did, he read the article. It spoke of the man restraining a burglar, and the burglar was injured after falling down the stairs several times.

"I remember, now," his grandfather said softly. "Yes, Mr. Boyd told me about it. The young man had screamed about the war trophies, about Mr.

Boyd being a war-lover."

"Do you think he went back and stole the war trophies, later on?" Jim asked.

"What do you mean?" his grandfather asked.

"Well," Jim said, "the article says the kid had stolen other stuff. And if he was freaking out about war trophies, what if he had stolen others? What if he was crazy and just had to steal those things? Didn't you say all of Mr. Boyd's stuff disappeared after he died?"

"Yes," he said, nodding. "Yes, it did. You're right, James. What if the thief went back and stole everything? Skulls included."

"The article doesn't name the thief, though," Jim said with a frown.

"It wouldn't," his grandfather replied. "The boy was young, a teenager, according to Mr. Boyd. His name would have been kept confidential."

"How are we going to find out who he was then?" Jim asked.

"We'll need someone with access to old police reports," he said. He tapped his fingers on his cane. "We will have to speak with Brian, but it may be best to bring in the State Police Detective who came to the house."

"What?" Jim asked, surprised. "Do you really think a police officer is going to believe us?"

"All we can do is ask, James," his grandfather said gently. "And we won't be able to break into the police station to search for old records which may or may not exist."

Jim realized his grandfather was right, and he sighed. "Okay. Detective Brown just didn't look like he was the kind of person who believed in ghosts."

"You never know, James," his grandfather said with a smile. "Now, let's do a little more research and try to find anything else which may be useful."

"Okay, Grandpa," Jim said, and he turned back to the computer screen. He went back to the search results and started to read through them.

CHAPTER 27
RESISTING

Colleen Staples sat in her chair and looked at State Police Detective Dan Brown. On her lap, she held Romeo, her young Siamese cat. The animal purred steadily, and she scratched between his chocolate pointed ears. Detective Brown looked uncomfortable, his tea cup exceptionally small in his large hands. He smiled at her, and she returned it.

"Mrs. Staples," he said, setting the porcelain down and picking up his pen. He held it above his notepad, ready to write. "I was wondering if you might be able to tell me what's been going on over at the First Church."

Colleen looked at him for a moment.

She had never in her life been a busy body. Other women had indulged themselves in gossip, but Colleen never had. Gossip hurt, and it was just as bad to cause pain with words as it was with something far more physical.

"What exactly are you inquiring about?" she asked. Romeo rolled on her lap and exposed his stomach. Absently, she moved her hands and rubbed under his arms and the fur on his chest.

"Well," Detective Brown said, "you were the one who discovered the two boys who had been injured. I was wondering if perhaps you knew about any other curious happenings in the Church."

"I don't pay any mind to things I haven't seen or heard myself, Detective," she replied.

"Of course not," he said, smiling broadly. "Is there anything, however, you might have seen or heard which would qualify as curious?"

"Not particularly," Colleen said easily. "Everything seems to be in order, except for the terrible accident which befell Matthew and Carlton."

"Was it an accident?" Detective Brown asked. "I thought perhaps it was another boy."

"Another boy?" Colleen asked. "No, no I don't believe so."

"Not James Bogue?" he said.

Colleen gave him a stern look, one which used to send her husband Kenneth out of the room.

It caused the detective to clear his throat and lower his eyes.

"I don't believe James Bogue would be capable of such an act," she said firmly. "He's a quiet boy, and I've seen bigger boys pick on him. He always stands up for himself, and for others. He might punch and kick, but I know he would never have put out the eyes of Matthew and Carlton. No matter how angry he became."

"So nothing stands out as strange?" Detective Brown asked. "Nothing at all?"

"I can't think of anything out of the ordinary, Detective," she said. "Why all of this interest? Have you found who hurt the boys?"

"No," he said, putting his pen away. "We had an officer killed in the Church yesterday."

Colleen's breath caught in her throat, and Romeo sat up on her lap. The cat looked over the edge of the table at the detective. "How?"

"We're not quite sure," Detective Brown said. He stood up and put away his notebook. "Thank you very much for the tea, Mrs. Staples."

"You're welcome," she replied. She set Romeo down on the kitchen floor and slowly stood up.

Detective Brown took out a business card and handed it to her. "Please, if you think of anything, anything at all, call me."

She nodded as she took it from him. "I will, Detective."

"Thank you. I'll show myself out. Have a pleasant evening."

Colleen smiled and watched him leave. The side door clicked loudly, and she walked over to it. She turned the deadbolt and glanced out the side window. A few police cruisers and a single, dark blue van remained parked in front of the Church. She watched Detective Brown walk to the back, past the burial ground, and into the building.

Colleen went back to the table, gathered her cup and the detective's. She brought them to the sink, rinsed them out and set them aside to be washed later. She then looked down at the floor.

Romeo lay on his side. His tail twitched as he watched Violet enter the room. The slightly younger female did so cautiously, fully aware of where Romeo was, the air of playfulness given off by his twitching appendage.

"Romeo," Colleen said sharply. "You leave her alone. She's allowed to eat, too."

Romeo rolled onto his back, looked at Colleen and yawned. Violet took the opportunity to steal past him and make it safely to the food and water dishes. The Siamese looked from Colleen to Violet, twisted and got up, and with a final, disdainful glance at both of them, wandered off.

A moment later, one of the other cats cried out, and Colleen saw Lily run past the open doorway for the stairs.

He's a brat, Colleen thought as she walked back to the side door. *Of course, you've never had a Siamese who wasn't.*

She pulled the curtain aside and caught sight of Detective Brown. He stood beside the police van, which had "State Forensic Unit" painted boldly across its side, and spoke with the driver. The other police vehicles had left, except for one unmarked gray sedan. A moment later, the detective stepped back, waved goodbye and turned away.

Colleen watched the van leave, and Detective Brown go to the solitary car. In a moment, he was in the gray vehicle and it, too, pulled away from the Church.

The police were gone.

Colleen let go of the curtain, put on her coat and hat and glanced over at Violet. The calico cat sat upright and politely cleaned her paw.

"Make sure they behave, Miss Violet," Colleen said.

The cat looked at her with an expression of bored incredulity, and then the feline went back to her bath.

Colleen smiled, opened the door, turned out the light and stepped out into the cold air.

The sun had started its descent, and the street lights flickered into life as she made her way to the back of the Church. As she got closer, she shook her head in anger.

The window to the right of the door was broken in and open to the elements.

Yellow police tape formed a cross over the window as well as the back door. Colleen paused at the base of the stairs and saw a dried splash of blood on the asphalt.

Reverend Joseph fell there, she realized. With a sigh, she shook her head, turned her attention once more to the Church, and climbed the steps.

Without the slightest regard for the authority of the State Police, Colleen pulled the tape down and let herself into the office.

The gasp which escaped her throat was completely involuntary, as was the mixture of horror and rage she felt.

The office was destroyed.

It looked as though a team of teenagers had tromped through the small room and ripped it apart, every last portion of it. She felt physical pain as she stepped further into the office. Papers littered the floor, drawers were piled haphazardly upon one another, and the furniture was thrown helter-skelter.

Colleen shook with rage, furious with the mess around her, and then she had a terrible, hideous thought.

Is there more? she wondered.

She picked her way through the mess to the door into the rest of the Church, and she opened it. A glance to the left showed nothing amiss, but to the right, she saw more yellow tape.

Across the kitchen doorway.

A frown creased her brow, and she left the office. She stalked down the hall and came to a stop in front of another yellow 'X'.

If the office was a mess, then Colleen wasn't quite sure how she might describe the destruction someone had visited upon the kitchen.

Every cabinet, every drawer, every container, even the refrigerator and the closet, had been emptied out. If an item could be broken, it was broken.

Glasses, plates, bowls, serving trays. All of them shattered, shards of porcelain and glass scattered amongst piles of sugar and salt. Loose tea and ground coffee was sprinkled about, as though someone had attempted to decorate with the ingredients.

Puddles formed from water, soap, milk, and creamer lay in the low points of the old tile floor. Packages of goldfish and saltine crackers had been opened and crushed. Flatware had been bent and twisted.

It would take Colleen hours to clean it all.

Hours.

I'm not waiting until tomorrow, she thought angrily. *If they even let me come in tomorrow. No, they must have gathered their evidence. I can't see it any other way.*

She turned around, stepped back into the hall and took off her winter hat and coat. She put them away in the coat closet and then turned her attention back to the kitchen.

Something rattled in the basement.

Colleen straightened up and paused.

The sound of voices drifted up through the floor vent to her.

Are the police still here? she wondered. The place was filthy and needed to be scrubbed. If the police decided she shouldn't be there, well then they would have a fight on their hands. The upkeep of the Church was her responsibility.

She made her way to the basement door, opened it and started down the long, narrow stairs.

And what type of animal vandalizes a Church? she asked herself. *How wretched must such a person be?*

At the bottom of the stairs, she paused to turn on the lights, passed by stacks of old wooden folding chairs and made her way through the basement.

The voices came from the furnace room.

And there was no light to be seen from beneath the closed and locked door.

In fact, she had needed to turn the lights on when she came down.

The ghosts, she realized.

The voices in the darkness spoke a language she couldn't understand.

The anger she felt about the mess in the kitchen and the office was drowned beneath a sudden, horrific wave of fear.

These ghosts had blinded the boys. Killed a police officer.

Colleen gasped and staggered. When she regained her balance and looked ahead, she saw she was no longer alone.

Two men stood before her. Young Japanese men, clad in khaki uniforms stained with dirt and blood. One of them snapped a question at her, and she couldn't answer.

She didn't understand them.

The other asked another question.

"What have you done to the Church?" she demanded. "Where is Miles?"

Both of the men looked surprised, and then they laughed. One of them said something and the other laughed harder.

"Who do you think you are?" Colleen said, crossing her arms over her chest. "You cannot simply come in here and do as you please. You hurt those boys, and you killed a police officer. You are not, I believe, Christian men."

The laughter faded, and the smiles vanished at the word 'Christian.'

"Now you listen to me," Colleen continued. "Miles Cunningham assured me, that you and your *friends* would be here to protect and care for my Church. He also assured me at least one of you would be able to speak English."

The two ghosts looked at each other and one of them repeated the word 'English.'

"Yes," she snapped. "Do either of you speak it?"

Neither of the men responded.

Anger boiled up within her. "This is completely unacceptable. How am I supposed to make certain you will be able to take care of this Church when I'm gone if I cannot even communicate with you."

Grim expressions appeared on the men's faces, and still they didn't respond. They merely watched her as one might watch a bug as it scrabbled across a hot surface.

"When I die," Colleen said, trying to control her anger. "You will be responsible for the protection of this Church, and neither those boys nor the police officer deserved what you did to them. This is not how you will behave in the future, am I making myself clear?"

"Die," one of the ghosts said.

In response to her question both men drew knives from their waists. Long knives, the edges of which gleamed curiously in the pale glow of the overhead lights.

The knives, Colleen suddenly understood, were for her.

She took a single step back, and the men spread out.

The men's faces lacked all emotion. Their knives were held out and again she was asked a question she didn't understand.

Before she could answer, however, the man on the left stepped gracefully in. His movements were delicate, with all of the coordination of a professional dancer, and she barely felt the bite of his knife as he slipped it into her side.

Colleen gasped at the intense pain and the second man jumped in. His knife joined his comrade's. The first man leaned in and whispered a single word to her.

"Die."

And both of the knives twisted at once.

CHAPTER 28

IN THE RIVERWALK

Brian finished the last of his salad, set his fork down and drank some water. He really wanted a little whiskey to wash the meal down, but he would have to wait until he was back in his hotel room for it.

The waiter, a pimply faced young man named Tim, came over and cleaned away his dishes.

"Do you want anything else?" he asked Brian.

"Coffee, please," Brian said with a smile.

"Decaf?" Tim asked.

"God no," Brian said, laughing and shaking his head. "I am a finely tuned caffeine filtration system. Decaf just gums up the works."

Tim grinned and nodded. "Okay. Cream or sugar with it?"

"No thank you," Brian said. "Just plain old black coffee."

"Okay." Tim left with the dirty dishes and Brian glanced at his phone on the table.

No new text messages. No new alerts.

Shane Ryan was due to arrive in the next fifteen to twenty minutes if traffic hadn't been too heavy.

The door to the coffee shop opened, and Brian looked up.

Luke, Jim, and the Reverend walked into the shop.

Looks like the start of a joke, Brian thought, trying not to chuckle. *A teenager, a blind man, and a Reverend all walk into a coffee shop.*

Jim and the Rev waved to Brian, and he returned it.

"Just the man we were looking for," Reverend Joe said when they reached the table.

"Take a seat," Brian said. "Why didn't you text or call me?"

The Reverend's face reddened with embarrassment as the three of them sat down. "I'm ashamed to say I seem to have misplaced my phone. It might be at home, or in the car, but I cannot find it."

"Did you call it?" Brian asked.

Jim answered for the Reverend. "I already asked him. Guess he forgot to charge it, too."

Reverend Joe nodded in agreement.

"Well then," Brian said, but then he paused as Tim returned with his coffee.

"Would any of you like something to drink?" the young man asked.

"Just water for me, please," Reverend Joe said.

"Coffee, black, please," Luke answered.

"The same please," Jim said.

Luke tilted his head slightly towards his grandson and asked, "Are you sure? You may be up all night."

"I'm sure," Jim answered.

Tim smiled. "Alright, then. Water, two coffees. Got it."

"So," Brian said after Tim left. "What is it you wanted to talk to me about?"

"James and I may have found something," Luke said. "We read about Mr. Boyd having caught a young man trying to burglarize his house. And, from what I remember when speaking with Mr. Boyd, the boy was intent on getting into the trophy room."

Brian looked at Luke. "You think maybe the kid went back? After Mr. Boyd died?"

Luke nodded.

"When he was arrested," Jim said, "the police reported they had found other stolen items in his room at home. Maybe he couldn't help himself. Maybe he had to go back."

"Okay," Brian said, nodding. "Let's say he went back. He learned, somehow, about Mr. Boyd dying. He figured out he could get into the trophy room and steal the stuff. Did you find out who this kid was or anything?"

Luke and Jim shook their heads.

"It's why they came to me," the Reverend said. Again they paused as Tim returned with the drinks. Once he left, Reverend Joe continued. "Luke and I believe we need to go to the police."

"The police?" Brian asked.

"Yes," the Reverend said. "We need to show them the phone, to begin with. Also, I think, and Luke agrees, Detective Brown might be able to help us look at the file with the thief's name."

Brian rubbed his jaw for a moment, took a sip of coffee and said, "You know you may well be arrested for withholding evidence in an investigation?"

The Reverend nodded. "I have thought of it. However, I don't really see how we can find out what we need to about the young man, any other way."

Brian frowned. "We could always see if we could make contact with Mr. Boyd again."

"No," Luke said, shaking his head. "Mr. Boyd never knew who the thief was. The police never told him. They were worried he might retaliate. He hurt the young man. A lot."

"We're taking a big chance here," Brian said shortly. He looked down into the dark liquid in his mug. "I'll be surprised if the police believe the video is real. Kids are pretty adept at all sorts of tech stuff nowadays, and I think you might be biting off more than you can chew. Also, there's no guarantee the detective will even be able to access the records we need."

"Still," Luke said, "I'd like for us to try it."

Brian looked again to Reverend Joe and the man nodded.

Brian sighed. "Okay. I'll do a little more digging myself. I'd like to find an alternative to the detective, if possible. Just in case he doesn't work out."

The Reverend looked relieved. "Excellent. Well, Luke, what should we do from here?"

"We'll go back to my apartment," Luke said. "I'll call Detective Brown and ask him to meet with us. We can work it out from there. First, though, let's finish our coffee."

"An excellent idea," Brian said, and he lifted his mug. The four of them drank in silence, and Brian wondered where Shane was.

CHAPTER 29
A CURIOUS SURPRISE

Dan Brown's work phone rang, and he looked at it. After the second ring, he reached out and answered the call.

"Detective Daniel Brown, New Hampshire State Police," he said.

"Detective," an older man said. "This is Luke Allen."

Dan blinked, and he recognized the name.

"Mr. Allen, sir," Dan said with a smile as he sat back into his easy chair. "What can I do for you?"

"I was wondering if you could come to my apartment," Luke said. "I have something you may want to see."

It took a moment for the statement to register and Dan wondered what a blind man could possibly show him.

"I'm sorry, Mr. Allen, I don't mean to sound crass, but aren't you blind?" Dan asked.

Luke chuckled. "I am. And I don't mean to sound trite, but, well, I have something here, and the Reverend Malleus and I both feel like you should see it."

Dan straightened up. "What do you have, Mr. Allen?"

"I have a phone," Luke said, "and while I obviously haven't seen what's on it, the Reverend has."

"A phone," Dan said. "Matt Espelin's phone?"

"Yes, sir."

Dan tried to contain his excitement. "It shows what happened to Carlton? It shows who did it?"

"Yes," Luke answered.

Dan reined in the urge to tell the man to bring the phone directly to the

Keene Police station. "You said you'd like me to come over?"

"Yes, sir," Luke said, "if it isn't too much trouble?"

"Not at all," Dan said excitedly. "I live in Falstead, just on the other side of old Mason. I should be there in about half an hour."

"Excellent," Luke said, relief thick in his voice. "Now, Detective, I've heard the recording. I can only imagine the visual portion of it is just as terrible."

"I need to see it," Dan said. "I'll be there soon."

He ended the call and stood up. Part of him raged against whoever had kept the phone out of evidence. But he needed to get it back, the sooner the better. If there were a case which had to be built against someone, it might be a little tough, but he was sure they could work around it.

Barely able to contain his excitement, Dan quickly got ready, worried the phone might disappear again.

CHAPTER 30

MEETING SHANE RYAN

Brian patted the pockets of his shirt and realized he hadn't brought his cigar or lighter with him from the hotel. He sighed, dropped his hands back to his lap and shook his head.

"Brian Roy?" a voice asked.

Brian looked up, surprised to see a man his own age across the table from him.

He hadn't heard the man approach or even enter the coffee shop.

The man was bald.

No, Brian realized. *He's completely hairless.*

Yet even as the thought crossed his mind Brian stood up and offered his hand. The man shook it warmly and sat down.

"I'm Shane Ryan," Shane said as Brian returned to his own seat.

"A pleasure, Shane," Brian said. "And I really appreciate you coming up here."

Shane grinned and shrugged. "Not a big deal. And, seriously now, how could I resist? You've got two ghosts who speak Japanese?"

"I do," Brian said.

"See," Shane said, smiling, "how can I not come up here for Japanese ghosts? When, in New Hampshire, am I going to get an opportunity like this one?"

Brian chuckled and shook his head. "I don't know."

"Exactly," Shane said. "So, why don't you give me the info on what's going on here?"

Brian did.

He told Shane everything from the two teenagers being blinded to the information about Mr. Boyd. He made sure he didn't leave out any part of the story.

When Brian had finished, Shane signaled to Tim and ordered a cup of coffee.

"I'm glad I came," Shane finally said. "This is going to be interesting. So, the others are with the detective right now?"

"I'm not sure," Brian answered. "If they're not, I'm sure they will be. The police won't waste time getting their hands on the other phone."

"I wish you still had it," Shane said. "I'd like to hear what the first one was asking about."

"I downloaded the video," Brian said.

Shane grinned. "Of course you did. Is it at your hotel?"

"Yeah," Brian answered. "It's just up the street."

"The Holiday Inn?"

Brian nodded.

"Good. I got a room there," Shane said. "Figured I might be here a day or two. Didn't want to have to drive back and forth from Nashua."

"Good call."

"After my coffee, can we go up there and take a look at it?" Shane asked.

"Of course," Brian said. "I'd love to know what the ghost was saying, too."

"Sounds good to me," Shane said.

A moment later, Tim arrived with Shane's drink.

"How'd you get into the ghost business?" Brian asked.

"Grew up in it," Shane replied. "And not in a good way. Haunted house."

"Bad?" Brian said.

"It had its good days and its bad," Shane said. "Too many bad ones, though. My therapist says I suffer from PTSD because of the house. I asked her if it was the house or the combat I saw in Afghanistan. She said the early childhood trauma trumped the adult issues."

"What do you think?" Brian asked.

Shane shrugged. "Not sure what to think. She's nice enough, but, hey, she works for the Veteran's Administration. Pretty sure they don't want to cough up any cash for PTSD. I had a hell of a time getting them to pay for my partial disability."

"What do you mean?" Brian said, leaning back in his chair and crossing his arms over his chest.

Shane grinned. "I told them I had bad knees, a bad back, and tinnitus."

"Infantry?"

"Did a lot of translating, especially on the ground," Shane said. "But I spent way too much time walking around the Afghanistan with a full pack. Anyway, my first evaluator said there was no evidence of combat-related injuries."

"Seriously?" Brian asked. "Hold on, why am I even surprised? What happened?"

"I grabbed a box of copy paper nearby, told him to carry it around the building for as long as he could and then to come in and tell me how his back and knees felt." Shane took a drink of his coffee. "He called the VA police, they came in, a supervisor came in, and I told them what was going on. The super, he looked at my record, looked at the evaluator and told him to get out. I'm on thirty percent disability now for my knees and back, plus the tinnitus."

"I avoid the VA because of their attitude," Brian said.

"You were in?" Shane asked.

"Ten years. Army. Forward observer," he answered.

Shane raised his mug to him. "More power to you, my friend. That's a hell of a lot of time out in the field."

Brian laughed, and Shane grinned before he finished his coffee. He motioned for Tim, and the waiter hurried over with the bill. Shane looked at it, nodded, and pulled a ten-dollar bill out of his front pocket.

"Keep the change, kid," Shane said, standing up. "I'm all set if you are, Brian."

Brian stood as well and slipped his book into the pocket of his sweatshirt. "I am."

They left the shop together and made their way up the street to the

Holiday Inn. Neither of them spoke as they entered the hotel and rode the elevator up to Brian's room. Once they were inside and the door was locked, Brian turned on his laptop and glanced over at Shane.

The man stood in front of the window and looked out at the wooded landscape.

"You okay?" Brian asked.

"Hm?" Shane looked over at him. "Oh. Yeah, I'm fine. Every once in a blue moon, I wonder what it would have been like to have grown up without ghosts."

"Well, growing up without them treated me okay," Brian said, smiling.

Shane chuckled. "How'd you get into this business?"

"Bought an old farm house, out in Mont Vernon," Brian answered. "Problem was there were a lot of dead folks there. And one really rotten dead kid. Things sort of went from bad to worse."

"Yeah. They usually do," Shane said.

"How did you learn Japanese, if you don't mind my asking," Brian said. "Did you take it in college or in the service?"

"No," Shane said, grinning. "Neither of those. I've got this knack for languages. If I hear a language spoken, I pick it up really quickly."

"If you hear it?" Brian asked.

"Yup. I mean there are certain limitations," Shane said. "For instance, I'll never be confused for a native speaker of Japanese. I speak it extremely well, but since I didn't learn it when my palate was still forming, there are certain sounds I won't be able to produce properly. I can understand it like a native speaker, though. Chinese is still pretty rough for me. So many different dialects from city to city. Huge difference between Cantonese and Mandarin."

"Shane," Brian said, smiling. "I barely speak English, and it's my first and only language."

Shane laughed and stepped away from the window. "The video ready to roll yet, Chief?"

"Yup." Brian turned the laptop slightly, and Shane came closer. Brian hit 'play' and turned the volume up.

The boys laughed, and the ghost spoke.

"May I?" Shane asked, gesturing towards the laptop.

"Go for it," Brian said, nodding.

Shane paused the video, brought it back to the beginning, and started it again.

He did it twice more before he finally pressed 'stop' and straightened up.

"He wants to know where his friends are," Shane said. "He doesn't want to be alone."

"Damn," Brian said, dropping into the chair.

"You said there were two of them?" Shane said, sitting down on the edge of the bed.

"Yes," Brian answered, nodding. "But the ghost we spoke with, Mr. Boyd, he said there were six of them."

"And you have two?"

"Yeah."

"Where are the other four?" Shane asked.

Brian shrugged. "There's more, though."

"What?" Shane said.

"Mr. Boyd said the dead men like to have saké," Brian said.

"Okay. Fair enough," Shane said. "I mean, I prefer whiskey myself."

"Same here. The problem, though, is you have to have the skulls with you."

"Oh," Shane said. "And we don't know where the skulls are?"

Brian shook his head.

"Any idea of where the first two are?" Shane asked.

"Nope," Brian said, sighing. "Just somewhere in the church."

"But it still leaves four more to find?" Shane asked.

"And we need to find how the damned things are getting into the building to begin with."

"True," Shane agreed. After a minute, he said, "Do you want to go over there tonight?"

"What, to the church?" Brian asked.

"Sure," Shane said. "Why not?"

"No, not tonight," Brian said. "We'll have to clear it with the Reverend first. I really don't want to go in without his permission, or without anyone knowing."

"Yeah," Shane said, glancing at the laptop. "Our little, headless buddy there didn't seem like he was a particularly pleasant fellow."

Brian remembered the sight of the boy being blinded.

"No," Brian said. "He's not pleasant at all."

CHAPTER 31

IN THE BASEMENT

Miles was tired.

Exhausted, really.

But he had calmed Sato and the others down. He was still a little drunk, and foolishly he had driven back into the center of Rye.

Sato's skull was in the backpack, and he needed to get the ghost into the Church. He had even brought a bottle of saké for the others, too. They might not kill him, but they could certainly hurt him.

And he didn't want to be hurt.

The wheels of the car scraped against the granite curb in front of the Church, and he swore. A flat tire wouldn't help anyone at this point. Especially himself, if a cop rolled up and found him with a skull in the bag.

And where did you get this, Mr. Cunningham? He thought.

Well, officer, you see, there's a funny story about this skull, Cunningham thought.

I don't think there's anything funny about a skull.

Cunningham shook away the imaginary conversation and turned the engine off. He took the key out, accidentally dropped it, grumbled and picked it back up. Carefully, he tucked it into the front pocket of his jeans and grabbed the bag from the passenger's seat.

Good God, I really am still drunk, Cunningham thought as he stumbled out of the car. He looked around furtively and was pleased to find himself alone on the street.

It's three in the morning, he told himself. *Rye's dead at this time of the night. Day. Whatever it is.*

He closed the door gently, just enough so the interior light went out.

With cautious steps, he walked up the long path to the back of the

Church, and he nearly giggled as the Scooby Doo theme song leaped into his head.

He shushed himself and managed to remain quiet as he got to the side door.

It took him a minute to dig the key out and let himself in, but he managed.

Yet once he stepped inside, he froze.

The lights were on in the basement.

And he could hear voices.

A moment later though, he realized he could understand the words. Someone was speaking in Japanese.

Suddenly, his back became cold. Sato was awake.

Cunningham hurried down the stairs, missed the last two and sprawled into the room. He landed in a thick, dark liquid and his hands slipped as he struggled to get back to his feet.

Once he had gotten up, he looked around the room and came to a shocked stop.

The old wooden floor was coated with blood.

Far more blood than Cunningham had ever seen before. It was as though someone had taken buckets and mopped the floor in the dark, sticky fluid.

Bits of flesh, bone and offal decorated the walls.

A woman had been butchered.

Miles Cunningham knew the person had been female because the dead men had neatly arranged her clothes on the floor in the center of the room. They were stained with blood, but they were undeniably feminine.

Hideaki and Tenchi sat in a pair of folding chairs by the door to the furnace. They stared at him with hate-filled eyes, and suddenly he was quite glad he had bothered to bring a bottle of saké. The thought of another cup of the liquor turned his stomach, but it would be better to be sick than to be dead.

When Cunningham looked at them, he remembered his manners and bowed low.

Sato appeared at his side, and as Miles turned to look at him, the ghost struck him. The blow was cold and terrible. It sent Cunningham sprawling into the blood, and he closed his mouth in time to avoid a mouthful of foul remains.

"Fool!" Sato shouted. *"Why haven't you brought the others?"*

Cunningham got to his hands and knees. He kept his head bent, and his eyes averted.

"I cannot risk moving you all at once, Sir," Cunningham said, trying to keep the fear out of his voice.

"You shouldn't have moved any of us at all," Sato snapped, stepping closer. It was strange to see the ghost's boots so clearly, and yet observe how they left no trace through the blood.

"Did he bring us anything to drink?" Tenchi asked.

"Saké," Sato replied.

"Well, let him serve it," Tenchi continued. *"We're thirsty. The woman took a long time to die."*

"Who was she?" Sato asked.

"Practice," Tenchi answered. *"Now come, brother, let him serve us. The work was harder than it looks."*

"Get up," Sato snarled.

Cunningham hurried to his feet and raced to get the saké ready.

He ignored what little remained of the murdered woman.

He had his own life to save.

CHAPTER 32
A RIDICULOUS DISCUSSION

Luke Allen's apartment was small and austere, with no decorations of any kind.

Dan sat in an uncomfortable ladder-back chair while Luke sat on the couch. The Reverend sat in a kitchen chair which had been brought into the small parlor for the occasion. He held what looked to be the phone in question, and Dan resisted the urge to snatch it out of the man's hands.

Patience, Dan told himself. *Patience.*

"Detective," Luke said, "in a minute, the Reverend is going to hand you the phone, which I'm sure he's holding onto for dear life right now."

Dan nodded, remembered Luke couldn't see, and said, "Yes. He is."

"I know. His breathing hasn't slowed down since he heard you walking up my stairs," Luke said easily. "What you're going to see is going to be disturbing. I heard it all, and I know what screams of pain sound like, having voiced a few myself. I'm hoping you have an open mind, and after you see it, well, I have a favor to ask of you."

"Let's not get too far ahead of ourselves here, Mr. Allen," Dan said, putting on his best 'don't mess with me, I'm a trooper' voice.

Luke merely smiled at the tone. "I'm not, Detective. I'm just letting you know what I'm hoping for."

"Fair enough," Dan said.

"Reverend," Luke said. "Would you be kind enough to hand the phone to the detective, please?"

The Reverend nodded and wordlessly gave the cell to Dan.

Dan smiled his thanks, took the device and saw a video had been set ready to play. He glanced at Reverend Joseph and the man nodded.

With a shrug, Dan started the recording.

When it had finished Dan's heart thumped loudly against his chest. Silently, he played it again.

And again.

And again.

Finally, he pressed 'stop' and put the phone down on his lap.

"Is this real?" he asked after a minute. He knew it was. Felt the horrific truth of it deep in his gut. But still, he needed to ask.

"Yes," the Reverend answered.

Dan didn't want it to be true. He wanted it to be a terrible joke. Some sick prank.

There were two boys, blinded by something, and in the hospital. And Officer Raelynn was dead.

The situation was a serious one, and Dan needed to think out of the box.

The kids had said it was a ghost who had blinded them, Dan remembered.

And why would the teenagers lie about it? There would have been every reason in the world to tell the truth. Who's going to lie about being blinded by a ghost?

There was also no reason for grown men to tell the same lie, if indeed it was a lie.

Dan sighed, shook his head and looked up at Luke and asked, "What's the favor?"

"We believe we may know how to stop anything else bad from happening," Luke said carefully.

"What do you need from me?" Dan asked.

"Years ago," Luke said, "back in nineteen sixty-one, I think, Mr. Jonathan Boyd stopped an attempted burglary. The name of the burglar was never released. He was under eighteen."

"What does it have to do with this?" Dan said, gesturing towards the phone.

"The ghost you see in the film," Luke continued, "belongs to a skull that Mr. Boyd had in his possession. There were six skulls altogether. Yesterday, a second ghost appeared, which means a second skull was placed somewhere in the Church. Not only do we need to find the skulls in the Church, detective, but we need to find the skulls which haven't been brought in yet, as well."

"And you think the original burglar might have something to do with this?" Dan asked, not quite following Luke's line of reasoning.

"When Mr. Boyd died in January of nineteen sixty-eight, all of his memorabilia disappeared," Luke said. "I know because I asked around after I got home from Vietnam. The young man who was arrested was found, according to the newspaper, to have other stolen items."

"And you think he may have gone for Mr. Boyd's items after the man's death in nineteen sixty-eight," Dan said, nodding his head. "Yes. I can see how it can work. So, what happens after we find these skulls? Do we destroy them?"

"Not according to Mr. Boyd," the Reverend said, speaking up for the first time. "You see, we managed to speak with him in the morning, and he says the men like to drink their saké. And to be left alone, essentially."

Dan frowned, tapped on the phone with one finger and then he nodded. "Hold on, hold, Reverend. You're telling me you actually spoke with a ghost? Now listen, I'm having a hard enough time wrapping my head around the whole concept of ghosts. But are you saying you not only had a conversation with one, but the damned things drink, too?

"Yes," the Reverend said hesitantly. "It's difficult for me as well. But I can only tell you what I have been told, Detective."

"Alright," Dan said with a sigh, shaking his head "Alright. I guess it can't get any crazier, can it? I'll try and dig around. See if anything comes up. I'm not going to put this phone into evidence because, quite frankly, no one will believe what's on it. I'm still not sure I fully believe it myself, but I don't know if there's any other explanation for what was seen. What I do know, though, Reverend Malleus, is you need to keep everyone out of the Church. Do you understand?"

"Yes," the Reverend said. "We were already planning on doing so. We don't want anyone else hurt."

"No," Dan said, looking down at the phone on his leg. "No, we don't want anyone else hurt at all."

CHAPTER 33

JIM MAKES A FRIEND

Jim sat on the porch on the side of the house and watched Lisa get home from shopping. She caught sight of him on the porch and waved. He blushed and waved back as she smiled, grabbed a couple of grocery bags out of the trunk of her mom's minivan and helped to bring them in.

"She is a very pretty young woman."

Jim nearly jumped out of his seat and stared, surprised at a man who stood on the porch. Yet the man didn't look right, almost as if he was fuzzy around the edges.

Jim wondered if it was a trick of the light.

The man gave him a quick, awkward smile. "I am sorry. I certainly did not mean to frighten you."

Jim cleared his throat. "It's okay. Can I help you?"

The man shook his head. He was curious looking, almost a little flat, as though he was on the porch, but he wasn't on the porch.

The stranger flashed Jim a tight smile.

"Please forgive my awkwardness," the man said.

"Sure," Jim said, grinning. "No worries."

"I do not have any worries," he said, frowning. "Or are you saying you have no worries?"

Jim opened his mouth to answer, but the man continued to speak.

"Is it just a phrase?" the man asked.

"Yes," Jim nodded. "Just a saying."

The stranger nodded. "Excellent."

"May I help you?" Jim asked.

"Yes, please," the man said. "You, your grandfather, and Brian Roy, you are all going to attempt to restrain and detain half a dozen ghosts?"

"How do you know?" Jim said, confused.

"I know," the stranger said. "I must speak with Brian Roy, but I am not sure he will speak with me."

"Why?" Jim asked.

"I gave him a gift," the man said. "I do not speak the exact truth. I forced a gift upon him. Yes, it was forced. Therefore, it is not unreasonable to believe Brian Roy may not wish to speak with me. I have come, then, to see if you will ask him to speak with me."

"Um, sure," Jim said, feeling confused. "I don't know who you are, though."

"Oh yes," the man said, his eyes widening. "A name would help. I am sorry. I had forgotten. My name is Leonidas. But you can call me Leo."

CHAPTER 34

INTERRUPTED

Brian was almost asleep when there was a knock at his door.

He sat up and listened.

Wrong room? he thought sleepily, stifling a yawn.

"Hello? Brian?"

Damn it, he sighed. He got out of bed, pulled on his jeans and a tee shirt and walked to the door. He looked through the peephole and saw Jim Bogue.

Brian unlocked the door and opened it. "Hey Jim, everything okay?"

"Yeah, I guess," Jim said, shuffling his feet and looking embarrassed. "Someone asked me to speak to you because he's afraid you won't want to speak to him."

Brian frowned, confused. "Come on in. Take a seat, kid."

He stepped aside and let the teenager walk past him. Brian closed the door but left it unlocked. Jim went to the room's desk, pulled its chair out and sat down.

Brian went to the easy chair, grabbed a bottle of water off the small table and had a drink. "Sorry, I don't have anything to offer you."

"No worries," Jim said, smiling. "You know, I've never been in a hotel room before."

"What do you think?" Brian asked, chuckling.

"Just makes me think of Law and Order," Jim said, "like someone's hiding from the police."

"Well, thankfully, I'm not," Brian said. "Anyway, how'd you know where I was?"

"I figured you'd be here," Jim said. "Closest hotel. And I called my cousin, Freddy, he works in the lobby downstairs. He told me you were here and what room you were in."

Brian laughed and shook his head. "Fair enough. So, let me get this straight, someone came to you and asked if you could come speak to me?"

"Yeah," Jim nodded. "I was sitting on my porch, Grandpa and the Rev were upstairs with the Detective, and all of a sudden there was this guy there beside me. I never even heard him come up the stairs or anything. And our porch, it's really, really squeaky. He was kind of odd, though."

"How so?" Brian asked.

"Just, I don't know, awkward? Like he wasn't sure if he should say certain things. And he talked kind of funny."

"Did he have an accent?" Brian said.

"No, nothing like that. I mean," Jim paused, frowned and then he said, "It's like, instead of using a contraction, he uses both words. Instead of 'don't', he said 'do not.'"

Brian frowned. "Why is he afraid to talk to me?"

"He said he gave you a gift, but he isn't sure if you liked it," Jim said, shaking his head. "Like I said, he was a little strange."

"Did he tell you his name?" Brian asked, taking a drink of water.

Jim nodded. "He said his name was Leo."

Brian put the bottle on the table and looked at the young teenager. "I'm sorry, Jim, could you say his name again, please?"

"Leo," Jim said. "Well, Leonidas, but he told me I could call him Leo if I wanted."

"And he talked a little differently?" Brian asked softly.

"Yup," Jim said, nodding.

"And he wants to speak with me?" Brian said.

"He told me he did," Jim answered. He looked at Brian. "Are you okay? You look kind of sick."

"No, no. I'm okay. Did he say how he would get back in touch with you? Once you got my answer?"

Jim nodded. "He said he would stop by my house again."

"Alright," Brian said. He cleared his throat, had another drink and smiled tiredly at Jim. "When he visits, please tell him he can see me whenever he wants. I would be very happy to talk with him."

"Okay," Jim said, standing up. "It was really strange, you know."

"What was?" Brian asked.

"Talking with Leo. He knew all about the ghosts. How do you figure he knew?" Jim asked.

"Well," Brian said, shaking his head. "Leo just knows, kid. He just knows."

Jim shrugged. "Okay. I'll see you tomorrow then, Brian."

"See you tomorrow, kid."

Brian watched Jim leave and then, as the door clicked shut, he poured himself an extremely large shot of whiskey. After he had knocked it back, he set the glass on the table and got up. He went to the bed, picked up his phone and sent a quick text to Jenny.

Leo just got in touch through a kid up here.

As he waited for her response, Brian walked to the door, locked it, and wondered what it was Leo wanted to talk to him about.

I guess I'll know soon enough, Brian thought. He stripped off his clothes and laid back down in bed with the phone beside him.

CHAPTER 35

LIFE GETS DIFFICULT

For thirty-six years, the Board of Trustees for the First Congregationalist Church of Rye, New Hampshire had put forth a sincere effort to buy the property adjacent to the Church. The First Church's Trust owned the land between the Church and Mrs. Colleen Staples. She had willed her home and property to the Church, and upon her untimely death, the half an acre and the structure became part of the First Church's estate.

The Church also owned the Old Burial Ground, as well as the three acres of woods directly behind the burial ground, Mrs. Staples' home, and the Hurlington House. The Board of Trustees had long striven to obtain the Hurlington House, the ownership of which would have given the Church an entire block. A massive piece of property on which the trustees could build.

And the trustees succeeded.

The lawyer for the Church, Attorney Richard Slater, met with the representatives for the Hurlington House.

At three o'clock in the afternoon, Mr. Slater sat across a mahogany table from Attorney Rachel Madden and Mr. Eugene Hurlington. Mr. Hurlington was ninety years old and was tired of owning the Hurlington House, which offered sanctuary to men of dubious character. Eugene had inherited the home from his father thirty-seven years before, and he had enjoyed the constant offers from the trustees to purchase the property.

The week before, however, Eugene had been told he had pancreatic cancer, and it was time to get his affairs in order.

The Church, Eugene had thought, had been good sports over nearly four decades. He decided to give the Church his house, and the land around it. His only stipulation was that they name a building after him should they decide to tear down the structure and replace it with something else.

The trustees had readily agreed.

While Attorney Madden and Attorney Slater chatted about the intricacies of estate law, Eugene carefully and patiently signed the various papers which had been laid out before him.

When he signed the last one and lifted the pen from the page, he felt a cold shiver race through him and the earth shake slightly.

He looked up sharply to the two middle-aged attorneys. Neither of them showed any reaction, however, and so Eugene assumed he had imagined the sensations.

As he set the pen down, the world around the Church changed.

And while the attorneys felt nothing, others did.

Three dead Japanese soldiers who stood in the furnace room, felt their world expand.

The soldiers felt the change.

They made their way up the stairs, invisible to the world.

They went to, what had been, the edge of the Church's property, and they realized the invisible wall was no longer there.

Together, they stepped out onto the grass, crossed over it and stood before a large house. They looked at each other and smiled.

They could enter the new house.

They could hunt the living.

The men laughed happily and slipped into the building. They sought shadows in which to sit and wait for night.

For the darkness always amplified fear.

CHAPTER 36

THE REV RETURNS

Reverend Joe Malleus passed a beige Toyota Camry parked in front of the Church and drove his own car around back. He pulled it into the spot marked "Reverend Malleus" and shifted into 'park.' He left the engine running as he sat looking at the building.

Joe hadn't been able to sleep, and he decided, on a spur of the moment, to do some work. Inside of his office was a USB drive stored in his desk. He could use his fear-induced insomnia to finish the necessary tasks, because even though there was a pair of murderous ghosts, it didn't mean the life of the faithful stopped.

He still had to send the weekly newsletter to the printer, as well as forward the list of nominations for the next term of the Church's Board to all of the members on the mailing list.

Joe hesitated, a cold, uncomfortable feeling spreading through him. He walked away from the Church and went to stand in the long parking lot of Hurlington House. Joe felt a little better the farther he stood from the Church, which was a terrible sensation.

The Church was his spiritual home, the place where he had found sanctuary his entire life.

A shimmer of movement at the side of the Church caught his eye, and he saw three men step out from the shadows.

Three ghosts.

They were headless.

Joe stood frozen with fear, unable to look away as the dead walked towards him. His heart raced and the blood pounded in his ears. When they were a few feet from him, Joe was able to shake his fear and he turned to run back to his car. Joe took a single step towards it and screamed out.

A heavy, cold fist punched into the small of his back and knocked him down as a shot rang out. He couldn't move his legs, and he sobbed at the intense pain which pulsed through him. Joe tried to crawl forward, but all he could manage was a motion reminiscent of a fish cast onto land.

Footsteps approached, and Joe turned his head.

A small man, a real, live man squatted down beside him and looked at Joe sadly. "You weren't supposed to be here."

Joe opened his mouth to speak, but only a long, drawn out moan was voiced.

"I asked them to make it quick," the stranger said. "And they said they would. They already had a lot of fun with a lady earlier. I asked them to give you a minute, too, just to make sure you're right with God and everything. I hate like hell to think you weren't going to heaven, what with you being a Reverend and all."

Tears slipped out of Joe's eyes.

The man gave him a comforting pat on the shoulder. "It's alright, Reverend, it'll be painless from here on out."

With a nod, the stranger stood and stepped out of Joe's line of sight.

Something cold and round pressed into the base of his skull.

Our Father, who art in Heaven, Joe began.

A single shot ended his silent prayer.

CHAPTER 37

AWAKENED IN THE MORNING

Jim had forgotten to turn off his alarm.

He groaned and rolled over, reached out and slapped at his clock until he hit the 'snooze' button.

"Are you awake?"

Jim sat up and looked around.

Leo sat in the chair by Jim's dresser and Jim thought he could see the pattern of the upholstery through the man.

"How did you get in my room?" Jim asked, suddenly afraid.

Leo looked confused for a minute, and then he smiled. "Oh. I forgot to tell you."

"Tell me what?" Jim asked, wondering if his mom was still home or if she had already left for work.

"I am dead," Leo said.

Jim blinked, shook his head and said, "I'm sorry, what did you say?"

"I am a ghost. I am dead. My grandmother killed me."

Jim closed his eyes, rubbed them, and opened them again.

Nope, he's still here, Jim sighed.

"So," he said, "you're dead?"

"Yes," Leo said.

And he disappeared. A moment later, he was back in the chair.

"Oh," Jim said, shocked. "Oh. Wow. Um, yeah. You're dead."

"Yes," Leo said, nodding cheerfully. "Yes, I am."

Then Leo looked at Jim with some concern. "You are awake, are you not?"

"Yes," Jim said, not quite sure as to what to say or do. "Yeah. I'm awake."

"Very good. You were able to speak with Brian Roy last night," Leo said. It wasn't a question.

"I was," Jim agreed. "And he said he would be happy to talk to you. I guess I know why he was surprised when I said your name."

"Oh," Leo said, concerned. "He did not tell you I was dead."

"Nope," Jim said. "He left that part out."

"Perhaps he was concerned for you," Leo suggested. "Perhaps he did not wish to alarm you."

"He probably didn't think you would just show up in my room," Jim said.

"Probably not," Leo agreed. "I did introduce myself to you upon your porch. He must have believed I would do the same again."

Jim grinned. He liked Leo.

"More than likely, Leo," Jim said. "Can I ask you a question?"

"Did you not just ask me one?" Leo asked.

Jim thought he was joking, and then he realized Leo was being serious. "I did. How about, can I ask you some questions?"

"Of course," Leo said. He politely clasped his hands together on his lap and looked at Jim earnestly. "What questions do you have for me?"

"Well," Jim said, not quite sure how to phrase it. "Well, what's it like to be dead?"

Leo thought about it for a moment, and then he answered, "Much like being alive. Except I never get hungry. Or need to go to the bathroom. Or sleep. Sometimes I blink, though, and days go by."

"Oh," Jim said. "Were you afraid of dying?"

Leo shook his head. "Everyone must die. I did not want to die. But it was inevitable. I merely had to accept it."

"Did it hurt?" Jim asked.

"Extremely," Leo said. "I had never experienced pain similar to it."

"Oh," Jim said.

"Do not worry, though," Leo said, flashing him a tight smile. "Everyone has a different death. You may well experience a painless death. Or, on the other hand, you may die in excruciating agony."

Jim looked at Leo, and then he laughed and shook his head. "Thank you, Leo."

Leo smiled. "You are quite welcome. You know, I never asked your name. I am sorry."

"I'm Jim. Jim Bogue," Jim said.

Leo's smile grew bigger. "I am very pleased to meet you, Jim Bogue."

"Same here, Leo," Jim said. He stretched and yawned. "Do you want to go to see Brian together?"

"Would you go with me?" Leo asked, surprised. "I would greatly appreciate it, Jim."

"I'd be happy to," Jim said. "I just need to get dressed."

"Excellent," Leo said, smiling happily.

Jim waited a moment.

"Ah, Leo," Jim said, "do you think you could maybe leave the room for a moment?"

"Why?" Leo asked, confused.

Jim smiled. "I need to get dressed."

"What? Oh! Yes," Leo said. "I will be in the hall."

Jim watched as Leo stood up, turned and walked straight through the door and vanished.

Well, Jim thought. *He certainly is a little different.*

Jim got out of bed, dug some clothes out of the dresser, and wondered whether or not they would go to the Riverwalk again.

I hope Lisa's working, he thought. And he whistled as he dressed and thought of the young waitress.

CHAPTER 38

DETECTIVE BROWN DOES SOME DIGGING

Files on home invasions from the early nineteen sixties weren't the easiest things to find. Especially when they were from a place like Rye.

Dan found them, of course, but they had been misfiled under the town of Sandown, which made sense if you were lazy. Dan's first job as a teenager had been in a library, and he knew how people shoved books back wherever they felt like it.

The same principle worked with cops and files.

Especially old files.

And the files hadn't been in the Rye police department's repository either.

Nope. The city of Concord.

Dan had lucked out early in the search. An old and long since retired detective was looking at the updates in the Rye police station when he had overheard Dan asking about the files.

The man had remembered when everything had been transferred to the State capital right before a renovation.

More importantly, the retired cop had recalled how the files had never been brought back.

Dan's luck in regards to the Rye documents had continued to hold. When he made it to the repository in Concord, he had bumped into Mike Anderson, Dan's original ride-along partner and his daughter's Godfather.

Mike was working as the security guard in the repository.

A large coffee from Dunkin Donuts had served as an all access, no questions asked pass into every file Dan could ever dream of.

At twenty-three minutes past one in the afternoon, Dan had not only located the files in their curious location, but he had found the original police report.

Which, thankfully, included the name of the fifteen-year-old male perpetrator whom the homeowner had beaten the absolute hell out of.

George Montgomery of Ten Indian Rock Road.

Dan jotted the information down in his notebook, returned the file and made his way out to say goodbye to Mike.

"So," Mike said, putting down the magazine he had been reading. "Did you find what you were looking for?"

"I did," Dan said, grinning.

"What was it?" Mike asked. "You never told me."

"A name," Dan said. He tapped his notebook through his breast pocket. "George Montgomery."

Mike frowned.

"What?" Dan asked, some of his joy slipping away.

"George Montgomery," Mike said. "Not the George Montgomery, who lived in Rye, is it? Ten Indian Rock Road?"

"Yeah," Dan said. "Him exactly. Why?"

"You were a kid," Mike said, "but in sixty-eight, George Montgomery pulled a nutty."

"How so?" Dan asked.

"One night, after he pulled a double up in Dartmouth at the hospital, he came home and decided to do a little surgery on his mom." Mike shook his head. "It was the first case I worked on. The guy had turned his kitchen into a slaughter house. He literally cut her to pieces, Dan. I was so sick from what I saw, I couldn't eat any sort of beef for a few months. It was terrible."

"What happened to him?" Dan asked. "Is he in prison or the State mental ward?"

"Neither one," Mike said, shaking his head. "The knives he used on his mother he ended up using on himself. Committed suicide. Ritual suicide is what they said it was. Copied the way the Japanese do it. Slit open his belly, lots of other stuff, too. I still have nightmares about the house."

"Whatever happened to the house?" Dan asked. "It get sold off?"

"Nope. The place was paid for by the old man, who had passed away from cancer. Evidently George's father was worried about his wife and boy, so he set up a trust fund to pay the taxes. Last I knew, the place was still empty." He sighed, finished off the last of his coffee and looked at Dan. "Anyway, what were you looking into him for?"

"An old burglary, back in sixty-one," Dan said.

Mike nodded. "I remember hearing about it. George was some sort of super peacenik. Had a habit of breaking into veterans' homes and stealing any military stuff they had. Evidently, George decided to break into Mr. Jonathan Boyd's house. He picked the wrong house, though. From what I was told, Boyd caught George in the act."

"Boyd grabbed a hold of him, called the police, and then he beat the hell out of George until the police showed up. He knocked out some of the kid's teeth and broke an orbital socket. I think he may even have fractured a couple of George's ribs." Mike shook his head. "Wasn't even mad when he was doing it, so I was told. When my old sergeant asked Boyd why he had beat the kid so badly, Boyd had said the kid needed a lesson."

"Damn," Dan said, letting out a low whistle. "One hell of a lesson to be taught."

"Yup. So, did you want to talk to George about the Boyd case?" Mike asked.

"One similar to it," Dan lied.

"What, you upset someone and get stuck on the oldest of pointless cold cases?" Mike said, grinning.

"No," Dan said, forcing a chuckle. "Just something on my own time, for a friend. He's trying to track down a couple of German war trophies his father brought home, but went missing around the same time period. I was hoping to figure out what the hell happened to them."

"Too bad," Mike said sympathetically. "Let me know if you think of anything else you might want to look at. And hey, tell Sarah to drop her Godfather a line once in a while."

"I will, Mike," Dan said. He extended his hand over the counter, his friend sat behind, and they shook warmly.

"Be good, Danny," Mike said. "And you stop by soon, too. I get bored as hell here."

"Will do, Mike," Dan said.

With a nod to his old friend, Dan left the building, paused on the steps outside the front door and stretched.

Ten Indian Rock Road, he thought. *I wonder if there's anything still there.*

Dan let out a sigh and walked down to the sidewalk and towards the parking garage.

He needed to get in touch with the Reverend. They needed to figure out their next move.

CHAPTER 39

BAD NEWS

The morning sun was warm and fought back the chill of the wind.

Brian sat at a picnic table and smoked a cigar. Shane stood a few feet away with a cigarette and a cup of coffee.

"Seems like it's going to be a good day," Brian said, glancing at the clear sky.

"I hope so," Shane replied. "I'm not exactly thrilled at the idea of going to the Church. We need to make sure we have a definite exit strategy here, Chief."

Brian nodded his agreement.

He checked his phone to see if he possibly missed a response to the text he had sent to Reverend Joe, but he hadn't.

The side door to the hotel opened up, and a large man stepped out.

Luke Allen and Jim Bogue followed him.

Jim led his grandfather and the other man over to Brian. Shane turned, looked at them and remained silent.

Introductions were made all around. When it was done, the three new arrivals sat down at the table, and Brian asked, "Have any of you heard from the Reverend? I've been trying to reach him all morning."

"No," Luke said. "Jim has called twice, and so has Detective Brown."

"You must not worry about Reverend Joseph Malleus."

All of them turned toward the voice and there, under the tree beside a surprised Shane, stood Leo.

The curious little man, a strange little ghost, ever since his death at the hands of Florence at the Kenyon Farm, smiled warmly at Brian.

Brian smiled back, and with some trepidation asked, "Why don't we need to worry about the Reverend Joe?"

"He is with his God now," Leo said, nodding.

Oh, Jesus, Brian thought, sighing.

"Who are you?" Dan asked. "And what do you mean?"

"I am Leo," Leo said, slightly confused, as though Dan should have known his name. "And I mean the Reverend Joseph Malleus is dead."

Jim looked down at the ground, and Luke asked, "How did he die?"

"The dead killed him," Leo said. "Him and a woman."

"Hold on," Dan said, raising a hand and interrupting Leo. "What woman?"

Leo frowned. "I do not know her name. She was older. She liked cats."

"Mrs. Staples," Jim murmured.

"I think you are correct, Jim Bogue," Leo said, nodding. "Yes, I believe her name was Mrs. Staples."

"Was?" Shane asked.

"Yes," Leo said. "Was. She is dead, and she has moved on. Therefore, she must be referred to in the past tense, and not the present."

"They're both dead?" Dan asked sharply.

"Indeed, they are," Leo said. "She was butchered. Vivisected, really. They took an incredible amount of time with her, and I am really quite surprised they were able to spread her remains about as much as they were."

"Leo," Brian said.

"Yes, Brian Roy?" Leo asked, looking helpful.

"Please, not all of the details," Brian said. "Just the basics. How were they killed? Who killed them? When were they killed?"

"Ah, yes, of course," Leo said, nodding in understanding. "Mrs. Staples was tortured to death. The Reverend Joseph Malleus was shot in the back of the head at the base of the skull. It was not a real, physical pistol, I must add. It is merely a construct of the ghosts. It is the same construct with which they killed the policewoman in the church, and with which they shot Jim Bogue."

"Thank you, Leo," Brian said. "Now please, when were they killed?"

"Mrs. Staples was killed shortly after Detective Dan Brown left the church," Leo said, giving the detective a small smile. "For some reason, the Reverend Joseph Malleus went to the church in the very early morning. He nearly stumbled upon the carrier and then he ran afoul of the dead."

"The 'carrier'?" Dan asked. "Who, and what, is the carrier?"

"I do not know who he is," Leo said. "But he is the one who has brought the dead into the church, and who has hidden the body of the Reverend in the basement with the remains of the woman."

"Do you know why?" Luke asked. "Do you have any idea why he might have brought them to a church?"

"A church is sacred ground. It is sanctified," Leo replied. "I assume he is under the belief that once all of them are there, well, the church will somehow bind them."

"All of them," Luke said softly. "So he has another three skulls to bring, and they'll be bound?"

"They will not be bound," Leo said.

"Why not?" Shane asked, finishing his cigarette and putting out the butt before he stripped the filter down and tucked it into the front pocket of his sweatshirt.

"The Japanese practice Shinto," Leo said.

"What does that mean, Leo?" Brian asked, trying to remain patient.

"Shintoism is far different from Christianity," Leo said. "The rules which bind one do not apply to the other. The church will simply be a place for them to hunt. And they do enjoy hunting, by the way."

"Great," Dan said, tapping his fingers angrily on the worn wooden top of the picnic table. "So we have to get those six skulls and figure out what to do with them."

"Once we get them," Shane said, "it won't be a problem. You don't know him, Detective, but there's a man down in Nashua who specializes in problem ghosts. He and his wife will keep them sealed and away from the world."

"Really?" Dan asked, and then he shook his head. "Why am I even questioning this? I didn't even believe in ghosts until I saw the damned video footage."

Leo looked at Dan with a confused expression. "I do not understand why you would not believe. You are speaking to me, and I am a ghost."

Dan opened his mouth to respond, closed it, and shook his head.

"Let us remain focused," Luke said. "We have the six skulls to deal with from Mr. Boyd. Three of them are in the church, and three of them are with the carrier. Am I correct, Leo?"

"Yes," Leo answered.

"Very good. Am I also correct in assuming you know where the skulls are in the church?" Luke asked.

"Yes," Leo repeated.

"And if we bring saké, we should be able to secure the skulls?" Luke said.

Leo nodded. "You are correct."

"Do you know where the carrier lives?" Luke asked.

"No," Leo answered.

"I might," Dan said. "I did a little digging on the young man who broke into Mr. Boyd's house originally. He lived here in Rye, and in sixty-eight he murdered his mother and killed himself."

Luke turned toward Dan. "George Montgomery?"

Dan looked surprised. "Yes. George Montgomery. How did you know?"

Luke smiled. "It's a small town, Detective. Everyone knows everything about everyone. A murder suicide is big news, it sticks in a town's memory."

"It was George Montgomery," Luke said softly, shaking his head. "He was always a strange boy. His family's house is still empty, isn't it?"

"I'm not sure," Dan said. "I haven't had a chance to check it out yet."

"Do you think the skulls would be there?" Brian asked.

Dan nodded. "I read the detective's report on the Montgomery murder and suicide last night. Nothing was mentioned about skulls or war memorabilia in the list of items."

"His father was a bit of a paranoid when it came to atomic warfare," Luke said. "I am sure he would have built a bunker for the family and more than likely one which would have been hidden."

"So," Brian said, relighting his cigar, "we grab the skulls out of the church. We go to this Montgomery's house and find the other three, and we're all set. All of the dead are dealt with."

"No," Leo said. "Not all of the dead."

All of them turned to Leo.

The dead man looked serious. "All of those attached to the skull, yes. Those you will have taken care of."

"Wait," Jim said. "Leo, are you telling us there are more?"

"More ghosts, of course," Leo said, looking puzzled.

"Yes, more ghosts," Shane said, his tone filled with patience. "There are lots of ghosts out there, Leo. But are you saying, specifically, there are more ghosts from Montgomery's house?"

"Oh yes," Leo said, nodding. "A great many more. From what I have heard, the carrier has been hiding ghosts around Rye for years."

CHAPTER 40

STRATEGY

"I'm sorry," Shane said. "Did you just say he's been hiding the dead *all over New Hampshire?*"

Leo nodded. "I did."

"Wow," Jim said, shaking his head. "It's like the worst Easter egg hunt ever."

"Hold on," Brian said. "Right now, the only dead we need to worry about are the two who are killing and maiming people. Anything else is a task for another time. Deal?"

The others nodded.

Brian looked at Leo. "Okay, Leo. Does anyone know about the Reverend and Colleen, yet?"

"Yes," Leo said. "Due to the recent trouble at the church, two police officers went by to check on the building. The bodies were discovered."

"Well," Dan said, "at least the Church will be officially sealed off. In theory, we won't have to worry about anyone else getting in and getting hurt."

"It still leaves us with the need to find the skulls, however," Luke said.

"My suggestion," Dan said, looking around at everyone, "is to focus on where the rest of the skulls may be. We know there are three in the Church. I think I may know where the other three are.

Dan looked around. "More than likely, the other three are at Ten Indian Rock Road. I'd love to go there, but if the place is occupied now, then I'd have no legitimate reason to go in. I can't really take someone in for questioning about a murder committed by ghosts."

"What's your suggestion then?" Brian asked.

"Well," Dan said, "I can't really tell you to go and watch the place. Or to see if the place is empty. Or to see if you can get in there. Telling you to do those things would be wrong. Criminal even."

"Ah," Luke smiled. "Since our friends here would obviously never do such a thing, Detective, what might your plans be?"

"Mine?" Dan said. "Mine will be to find out whether the house in question was ever sold, or rented, or whatever. I believe I have your number, Luke, and we can figure out the communication logistics after."

"Fair enough," Brian said.

"I have to go," Leo said suddenly.

And then he was gone.

"Jesus Christ," Dan muttered.

Shane lit a fresh cigarette and looked at the detective. "Don't worry, you'll get used to it."

Dan shook his head. "I don't want to."

CHAPTER 41
PANIC SETS IN

Miles Cunningham threw up in his bathroom and gripped the sides of the toilet tightly.

He wasn't drunk anymore, and he remembered vividly what the dead had done to the old woman.

The image of the woman's blood, caused Miles to vomit again.

He spit out a few mouthfuls of bile, sat back and wiped his mouth with some toilet paper.

Three more skulls, he told himself. *Just three more of them to move, and then I'll be fine. Everything will be fine.*

A dry heave ripped through him, and he felt as though his throat would burst from the effort.

With a grimace, Miles got to his feet, flushed the toilet and rinsed his mouth out with cold water. A glance in the mirror showed he looked as haggard as he felt. He splashed some water on his face, wet his hair and took a cautious sip from the tap.

When his stomach didn't forcefully reject it, Miles drank a little more.

The morning sun filtered in through the lace of the old curtains and he glanced out at the back yard. A squirrel ran past, and Miles smiled.

It's going to be okay, he told himself.

He dried his face, folded the towel neatly and hung it back up on its bar. He left the bathroom carefully. He didn't particularly want to run into any of the Japanese soldiers. They had gotten a good drunk on, but they were volatile. They could sleep for days. Or they could be in the front room, ready to harass him. Threaten him.

Miles went into the kitchen and got a few saltines out of the cupboard.

He nibbled on them as he went into the front room.

No ghosts.

He sat down on the floor and leaned against the wall. He looked at the television and wondered if he should put a movie on.

Finally, he shook his head and focused on the crackers. He needed to wait for his stomach to settle before anything else.

Miles closed his eyes and rested his head against the wall.

How am I going to get the skulls in there? He thought. *The place is going to be crawling with cops now. They're going to rip through the place looking for evidence.*

Miles' head snapped up, and his eyes opened.

Evidence, he thought. *Oh, sweet Mary Mother of God, evidence.*

He hadn't been careful. Not the last time. Sato had made him upset, nervous.

Miles had been sloppy.

Oh God, Miles thought, his heart hammering away in his chest, *what did I leave behind? Fingerprints? Hair?*

It doesn't matter, a small voice said. *It doesn't matter if you did. You can explain it. You were there. Even your boss can say you were. You did the duct work.*

But I did the job months ago, Miles told himself.

Doesn't matter, the voice said. *Not at all. Trace evidence survives.*

I don't have an alibi! There's blood all over everything!

Start cleaning, the voice said in a matter of fact tone. *Start scrubbing. You have plenty of time, just don't waste it.*

Miles nodded.

He got to his feet, ignored the ominous rumble in his stomach, and stripped naked in the family room.

He needed to destroy everything he wore. Scrub everything else. He needed to be *clean.*

CHAPTER 42

LOU'S LUCK

Lou Hanson had lived in the Half-Way House ever since he had finished his time in State. He had spent thirteen years at the correctional facility for an armed robbery he vaguely remembered.

Hell, Lou couldn't remember most of the years between nineteen eighty-seven and nineteen ninety-seven. The only reason he remembered the end of the century was because it was through forced sobriety.

Solitary confinement was a tough place to kick a heroin habit, but he had.

Lou picked the habit up again within three weeks of being out. He still liked to get high, although not as high has he used to.

The past six years at Half-Way House had been a little rough. It was tough to get high with the staff always on the lookout. They even checked for needle marks, which meant Lou couldn't shoot up.

He snorted the heroin, but it just wasn't the same.

Then Winnie had moved into the House.

Winfred Beauregard. Fifty-five years old with a strong old habit. He even shot up.

In the ear.

Winnie had shared the secret, too.

Lou patted the pocket with his needle and kit and heroin, to reassure himself everything was still there.

It was.

Now Lou just needed a place where he could shoot up.

The burial ground, he thought, a smile appearing on his face. *The burial ground behind the Congregationalist Church.*

He had walked by the Church earlier in the day. The place had been crawling with cops. Word got to the House about how the Reverend and the caretaker had been killed.

Lou felt bad about it. Both of the dead people had been nice to him and the other guys he lived with. Lou had seen the Reverend down at the soup kitchen a few times, and the caretaker always let him go into the Church and warm up when it was cold out.

Lou, since he was still sober, managed to avoid the police. They didn't see him as he slipped into the back of the burial ground, and found a good spot behind a huge marble marked with the name 'Grenier'.

The moon edged out from behind a bank of clouds and cast an eerie, silvery light onto the old graves.

Lou didn't worry about any ghosts.

He didn't believe in them.

When you were dead, you were dead as far as Lou was concerned, so there was nothing to worry about.

With a happy sigh, Lou got comfortable against Grenier's stone, ignored the chill in the air and pulled his kit out of his pocket. He hunched over the spoon and went about the grotesque ritual of cooking up his heroin. Lou made sure to hide the flame of the lighter as much as possible, and soon he had the hypodermic loaded.

His hand shook with excitement.

The idea of a mainline high brought tears of joy to his eyes, and he paused to wipe them clear.

Metal scraped against stone.

Lou froze, and his heart thundered.

Oh Jesus, not now, please not now, he thought. He waited a moment and when he didn't hear anything else he found the sweet spot and gave himself a boost. As he depressed the plunger he felt the heroin slide into his bloodstream and he let out a long, happy sigh.

He gave it a few seconds before he took the needle out.

Lou closed his eyes, put the needle on the ground beside him and waited.

Someone whispered, and Lou opened his eyes.

A man squatted in front of him.

An Asian man.

In a uniform of some kind.

Lou's mouth worked to form words, but his throat didn't supply any air.

The man looked at Lou inquisitively and then after a minute he reached out, picked up the needle and examined it.

Lou couldn't stop him. Not only was he unable to speak, he couldn't even move.

Did I get a bad dose? Lou thought. *Am I dying?*

The man leaned closer and Lou felt a painful chill brush his skin. Lou wanted to pull away, to leave, but he couldn't.

None of his muscles were listening. Nothing was obeying him.

The Asian man smiled, reached out and touched the side of Lou's face gently.

The cold was intense, as though someone had sliced open his cheek and packed the raw wound full of dry ice. Lou tried to scream and twist away.

Yet he was frozen in place.

The man's smile widened into a grin full of bright white teeth. He held up the syringe in one hand, peeled back Lou's right eyelid and slid the sharp medical steel into Lou's exposed eye.

Lou's throat almost burst with the shriek trapped within, and the stranger chuckled and pressed the needle deeper into Lou's eye.

Slowly, the man withdrew the needle and held it in front of Lou's undamaged eye.

Lou watched in horror as the man whistled cheerfully and brought the tip of the syringe ever closer.

And as the metal slowly punctured his eye, Lou found he was able to scream.

CHAPTER 43

DAN GOES TO CITY HALL

Rye, New Hampshire was several decades behind the curve when it came to technology and local government. While the taxes and other applicable bills were logged into a central system, there was no easy or digitized way to examine property sales and ownership in the town.

Dan was on his second cup of coffee, and the month of July for the year two thousand fifteen.

All of the previous months listed the house at Ten Indian Rock Road as still being in trust to the Montgomery family, although there were no more Montgomerys to own the land or the property.

Dan finished his drink.

July was a bust.

With a sigh, Dan pushed his empty cup away from him, stacked the useless file on top of a pile of the same, and pulled a manila folder labeled, *August 2015*, in front of him. He made his way carefully through each document. He read the pages and then he stopped on August seventh.

"Ten Indian Rock Road, care, and uptake of property taken over by Miles Cunningham, Montgomery cousin."

Dan sat back and looked at the entry, and he read it again.

Someone is living there, he thought, tapping on the page. *Someone found out what was there.*

And he's dumping it on the rest of us.

Dan took his notebook out and wrote down *Miles Cunningham, 10 Indian Rock Road, Rye, NH*, into it. He put the papers back in order, and then the files as well. Once he was finished, he put his notebook away, brought the paperwork back to the desk and signed out.

Dan walked out to his car, climbed in and drove over to the First Church. The place was sealed off, locked down.

He pulled into the parking lot and put the car in 'park.' Dan picked up the folder with Miles' name on it and wondered how the man was connected to the Church. What had brought him there in the first place?

Dan grimaced as a headache started at the base of his skull. With a frown, he checked the glove box for aspirin, didn't find any, and decided it was time to go to the Rye Police Station.

He needed to use the computer to see if Mr. Miles Cunningham, recently of Ten Indian Rock Road, had any sort of priors in the system. And they'd certainly have aspirin there. Dan needed to call Luke, so the blind man could get in touch with Brian.

Should have gotten his number, Dan realized. *Oh well, maybe Luke will give it to me. Or his grandson.*

With those thoughts in mind, Dan pulled into the Rye Police Station and got ready to go to work.

CHAPTER 44
SATO SEES AND KNOWS

Sato stood in the sun, imaging he could feel it. Wishing he was home, standing outside of the shrine instead of this foul church.

He watched as the strange automobile pulled in.

Curious, Sato walked up to it and looked in. There was a large man holding a folder, there was English written upon it. Sato squinted, then his eyes widened.

Miles Cunningham.

Sato tried to push himself into the man in the car, yet found resistance. The man was sober, unable to be possessed.

But for a moment, he was able to see where the man was headed.

The police station.

Sato backed out of the man, looked at the house which so recently became part of his domain, and smiled. With his own skull placed in the basement of the church, he could project himself out. How far out, he was unsure, but perhaps he could find out.

Sato went to the new house, looking for a drink.

CHAPTER 45

GOING FOR A WALK

Jim stood on his porch and listened to the robins as they sang in the yard. Lisa came out of her house, sat down on her front steps and put her face in her hands.

For a moment, Jim watched, and then he walked down his front steps and crossed the narrow strip of grass which separated the two properties.

"Lisa," he said cautiously.

She looked up. Eyeliner and mascara had run down from the corner of her eyes. Mixed with fresh tears, the black makeup made a mad pattern of twisted roots across her fine cheeks.

"Hey," Jim said, swallowing nervously, "I'm sorry, but, can I help you with anything?"

She looked at him for a moment and Jim almost took a step back, afraid she might yell at him.

Finally, she shook her head.

"No," she said, sniffing, letting out a small smile. "No. Timmy White just broke up with me."

"What?" Jim asked, surprised. "Seriously?"

She nodded.

"Why would he do something stupid like that?" Jim asked.

Lisa smiled sadly. "I don't know. I guess he doesn't like me anymore."

"How can anyone not like you anymore?" Jim asked. "I think you're great."

"Thanks," she said, wiping away the makeup with the palm of her hands. She looked at them, shook her head and then wiped them clean on the grass. "You're sweet."

"No," Jim said. "Not really. I just think anyone who would break up with you is an idiot."

Her smiled broadened, and she laughed a little. "Thank you, Jim. So, what are you up to?"

"Just waiting," Jim said. "I might have to go out with my grandfather soon."

"Where?" she asked.

Jim shrugged. "We won't know until we get the call."

"Sounds exciting," she grinned, and then she sniffled a little.

"It might be," Jim said. "Do you want to go for a walk?"

"To where?" she asked.

"Just up and around the burial ground," Jim said. "Can't get too close to the Church."

"I heard," Lisa said. "Terrible about the Rev and Mrs. Staples."

Jim nodded.

Lisa stood up. "I'd like to go for a walk, Jim."

"Really?" he asked, surprised.

"Yes, really," she said. "I've had a tough day, and you always make me smile. And plus it's really sweet of you to want to take a walk. Even if you don't think you're sweet."

Jim smiled. "Okay. Cool. Want to loop around, so we don't have to get too close to anyone's house, or possibly upset the police?"

"Sounds good to me," she said. "Do you need to tell your grandfather?"

"No," Jim said. "I told him earlier I might take a walk. Plus, I have my cellphone. If there's an emergency, he'll get in touch with me."

"I'm amazed your grandfather can do as much as he does," Lisa said. "I know he's been blind for a while, but still. It's crazy he can do all those different things."

"Yeah," Jim said proudly, "my grandfather's pretty awesome."

"Lead the way, Jim," Lisa said, smiling.

He did so. They walked quietly for a while. Together, they enjoyed the afternoon sun. Birds sang and occasional cars passed by. Neither of them spoke, and Jim waited patiently for Lisa to break the silence.

The walk really was for her. He knew it helped him to leave the house and wander, so he figured it might do the same for Lisa.

Eventually, they came to "Mirkwood," the path named for Tolkien's Middle Earth. It cut through a few acres of woods, which ran up to the back of the burial ground. They turned off the sidewalk and onto the worn dirt trail. Trash littered the ground every few feet, each item a reminder of how the path was about as far from "Mirkwood" as one could get.

"So," Lisa said, "who was the man you and everyone met with the other night?"

Jim paused before he answered. "Do you promise not to laugh?"

"I promise," she said.

"He's a ghost hunter," Jim said. "Did you hear about the ghosts in the First Church?"

Lisa looked over at him, as though to make sure he wasn't being silly. When she saw, he was serious, she said, "I had heard a rumor about a ghost being seen. Then Matt and Carlton got hurt, and the police officer died in there. Plus, the... the bad stuff with Mrs. Staples and the Rev."

Jim hesitated for a moment, and then he said, "It's the ghosts doing it all."

Lisa stopped and turned to face him.

"Are you serious?" she asked.

Jim nodded. "There are three ghosts in the Church now. Dead Japanese soldiers. They like to hurt people."

"Ghosts can't hurt people," Lisa said, shaking her head. But when Jim remained silent she asked in a low voice, "can they?"

"Yes," Jim answered. "They hurt me."

Her eyes widened slightly. "How?"

"They shot me," Jim said.

"Oh my God! Are you okay?"

"Yeah," Jim said, blushing slightly. "Um, do you want to see it?

"Is it... is it gross?" Lisa asked hesitantly.

"No," Jim said. "A little scar showed up hours after it happened."

"Okay," Lisa said. "As long as it isn't nasty looking."

Jim pulled his arm back into his sweatshirt and then freed his shoulder. Where the ghostly bullet had penetrated was a small, dime shaped scar. It was bluish in color and cold to the touch. His arm ached occasionally as he moved it. A reminder of what the dead could do.

"Oh my God," Lisa said, leaning closer.

Jim's heart skipped a beat as a sweet, delicate smell slipped over him. Lisa wore some type of perfume, the scent rich and enticing.

"Did it hurt?" she asked, looking up at him.

Jim nodded, swallowed drily and added, "It still hurts. What's really strange is how cold it is."

"What do you mean?" she asked, straightening up.

"The scar, it's cold when I touch it," he said.

"Oh wow," she whispered. Then Lisa looked at him and asked, "Would it be okay if I touched it?"

"Yeah," Jim said.

Cautiously she reached out and touched the scar.

The feeling was electric. There was pain at the slight pressure, but chills raced along his spine and goose bumps rose up on his arms. His heart skipped a beat.

"It is cold," she whispered. Her fingers lingered for a moment and then she drew her hand back.

She smiled shyly at him. "You said they shot you?"

"One of them did," Jim said, trying not to sound as excited as he felt. He put his arm back in his sleeve and tucked his undershirt in. "He pointed a gun at me and fired. Whatever it was, it hit me. When he went to shoot again, the second ghost stopped him."

Lisa reached out and took his hand.

They started to walk along the trail again.

After several moments of silence, she asked, "Is it safe to be on the other side of the burial ground?"

"I think so," Jim said, but doubt suddenly flooded him. "I mean, they didn't come out of the Church to chase me or anything. They stayed in the doorway. Why?"

"I just remember reading, somewhere, how ghosts can haunt more than a building," Lisa said. "I mean, they can haunt places and stuff. And I was thinking how the Church owns the burial ground."

"And it owns the woods here, and Mirkwood, too," Jim said softly.

"Oh wow, yeah, it does," Lisa whispered. "Do you think we should go back?"

"I think," Jim said, "since we're almost at the burial ground, it'll be better to get back home by going around the Church. I don't want to have to run from anything in the woods."

Lisa nodded. "Yeah, you're right. I don't want to be running from something through the woods either."

The trees thinned out, and the stones of the small graveyard behind the First Church came into view, as did the back of the building.

"Oh my God, Jim," Lisa said. She pointed with her free hand and said, "Look!"

Jim followed the line of her finger and saw a body.

An older man stripped naked.

Someone had cut out his eyes and crucified him on a stone cross. The man had been flayed as well. Strips of his skin were hung over stones, and dried blood was splattered across the same.

"We need to leave, Lisa," Jim said, squeezing her hand. "We need to get home, now! I have to tell my grandfather!"

Lisa nodded, and then she gasped.

A trio of men appeared in the open doorway of the Church.

Each of them carried a long knife and the one in the center pointed his at Jim and Lisa. The man spoke, and his comrades laughed.

The one on the right started down the stairs.

"Run!" Jim yelled.

He kept his grip firm on Lisa's hand and ran with her.

The men yelled as Jim and Lisa sprinted towards the Hurlington House.

Several shots rang out, and trees just beyond them exploded. Wood shards ripped through the air. Jim hissed as one tore into his cheek and slammed into his teeth.

And then they were behind the Hurlington House.

Screams of rage and fury chased after them.

Jim didn't look back, he and Lisa continued to run, straight for his porch and the safety of his grandfather's apartment.

CHAPTER 46

LUKE DRINKS TEA

Luke sat in the perpetual darkness which was his life.

He had a cup of tea in his hands, and he chased away thoughts of his ex-wife. Occasionally, it bothered him, the fact she had abandoned him and their daughter. How she had never known James and how wonderful he was. He couldn't understand how she had thrown all that away.

Luke sighed, brought the cup of tea to his mouth and blew upon the hot drink before he took a cautious sip.

I'm nearing my end, he thought.

The realization was sharp and sudden, but it was not painful.

Death was part of life. A new beginning, if the teachings of the Church were true.

He hoped they were, but he didn't worry too much about it. Either Luke would go to Heaven, if there was such a place, or he would not. If he dwelled on it, he would go mad.

So like the thoughts of his ex-wife, he pushed those of the afterlife away.

He relaxed and listened to the sounds of his house. Each noise comforted him, soothed him with its familiarity. Some nights he dreamed he could still see. But he was always back in Vietnam. Always on the morning when the sniper would rob him of his sight.

The door to the hallway on the first floor slammed and interrupted Luke's thoughts.

Two pairs of feet thundered up the stairs, and he recognized one of them as his grandson's. The other person was lighter.

A moment later, James knocked loudly.

"Come in, James," Luke said. He put his tea cup down as the young teen hurried in, his companion close behind him.

"Are you two alright?" Luke asked.

"Yes," James said, panting. "We're okay."

"Please, sit down," Luke said. He inhaled through his nose and caught the distinct scent of perfume. "And you as well, young lady."

"Wow," she whispered.

Luke recognized her voice.

He smiled. "It is not a magic trick, Lisa. I've simply had a long time to learn how to use my other senses."

He heard the two of them sit on the couch.

And close together, he imagined.

"Now," Luke said, "what has brought the two of you thundering up into my room?"

"The ghosts," James said quickly.

"James," Luke said sharply. "Did you go into the Church?"

"No, sir," James answered. "We took a walk through the woods behind the Church and came in behind the Old Burial Ground. We found a body. I think the ghosts tortured him to death. And then they came out of the Church, and they chased us to the edge of the property."

"To the edge of the property?" Luke asked, shaking his head. "They left the Church?"

"Yes, sir," James said, and Luke could hear the fear and exhaustion in his grandson's voice.

"Well," Luke said, forcing himself to smile. "You're safe now, James. You're here with me, and nothing is going to happen to either one of you, alright?"

The two teenagers answered 'yes' in unison.

"Good, good." Luke folded his arms across his chest and said, "Now, there's a fresh body, someone the ghosts killed?"

"Yes, sir," James said miserably. "It was terrible."

"Yes," Luke said softly, "I imagine it was, James."

Luke reached down to his left, found his cellphone and pressed redial. A moment later, Detective Dan Brown answered.

"Mr. Allen," Dan said cheerfully. "A pleasure. Everything alright?"

"I'm afraid not, Detective," Luke said. "My grandson just came in, and he has informed me that there is a mutilated body in the burial ground behind the First Church."

"Jesus Christ!" Dan snapped. He closed his eyes for a moment, then he opened them and said, "Okay. Alright, I'm in the Rye Police Station right now. I'll pass the word along. Is he alright?"

"Yes, thank you," Luke said. "Have you had any luck in regards to George Montgomery's house?"

"I have," Dan answered. "Turns out a cousin of his by the name of Miles Cunningham moved in recently. I'm going to do a little bit of digging to see if the man has any sort of record. Should only take about an hour or so. How about I meet you at your place at four o'clock?"

"Sounds like a good idea," Luke said.

"Will you do me a couple of favors?" Dan asked.

"Certainly," Luke replied.

"Could you make sure your grandson stays with you? More than likely, there should be a police officer at your house long before I get there to take your grandson's statement."

"I will. And the second request?" Luke asked.

"Contact Brian Roy, see if he can meet us at your house as well," Dan said. "I'd rather not meet in the Riverwalk and have anyone overhear our conversation."

"I agree," Luke said. "I'll have my grandson find Brian's number after this and give him a call."

"Excellent," Dan said. "I'll see you at four."

"Goodbye, Dan."

Luke ended the call and carefully returned the phone to the side table.

"James," Luke said.

"Yes, sir?" James asked.

"Detective Brown will be sending a police officer here to speak with the two of you, and I was wondering if you could find Brian's number and call him for me? I believe it's on the counter by the toaster," Luke said.

"Yes, sir," James said.

Luke listened as his grandson got up and went into the kitchen.

"How are you holding up, Lisa?" Luke asked.

Her voice came from the right side of the couch.

"I'm not sure," she said. "It doesn't feel like what I saw was real, even though I know it was."

Luke nodded. "Do you want to call your parents?"

"They're both at work, and they both had meetings today. I can't call when there are meetings," she said.

"You may have to," Luke said. "Police tend not to question teenagers without a parent present."

"I have it, Grandpa," James said, coming back into the room.

"Very good, James," Luke said. "Will you do me another favor and call him? The detective would like all of us to meet here at four."

"Yes, sir," James said.

Luke listened as the boy sat back down on the couch and dialed the number.

I wonder, Luke thought, *if George's cousin is as strange as George was.*

CHAPTER 47

ALEX CHARLES GOES FOR A DRIVE

Alex Charles, at forty-one years of age, had been a professional alcoholic since he was thirteen. Most days no one even knew. He had woken up at Hurlington House at four and pounded back the last half of a fifth of some cheap vodka. He was feeling pretty good, even with the headache which had started a little while before.

His thoughts felt fuzzy, as if they were crowded.

And he couldn't quite remember leaving his room and going down into the parking lot.

Even though he was drunk, and didn't recall why he was leaving, Alex didn't miss the lock on the truck door. Nor did he fumble with the ignition in the old Dodge Ram. Nope, everything went smoothly, like it always did.

The truck's engine turned over, the gears shifted, and he pulled out of the parking lot. Whistling to himself Alex drove happily down Main Street.

Sure, he almost hit a couple of parked cars, but hey, who didn't after a couple of drinks?

He fumbled with a cigarette, managed to get the truck's lighter pushed in, and jerked the wheel to the left in time to miss the mirror of a new Lexus as the car tried to pull out of a parking space.

"Jerk," Alex muttered to himself around his cigarette. He tried to inhale, remembered it wasn't lit, and stopped just in time at a red light. The lighter popped, and Alex pulled it out, lit the cigarette, and waved to the guy behind him who laid on the horn.

Yeah, green means go, but I'm busy, Alex thought. He dropped the lighter onto the floor, sighed, and eased into the intersection. The impatient driver jerked his Lexus to the left, and cut around Alex. The man gave Alex the

American, one-finger salute, and Alex waved again.

Whatever, Alex sighed, his head pounding with a vicious headache. The cab was cold too, and no matter how high he had the heat, the chill remained.

Tunes, Alex thought, suddenly. *I need some tunes.*

He leaned forward, turned on the radio, and for some reason he pulled down on the steering wheel at the same time. The truck jumped the curb, knocked the cigarette out of his mouth and onto his lap. Alex let out a shout of surprise and anger.

He slapped at the smoldering ashes on his jeans, then, without warning, his right foot stepped down hard on the gas.

Surprised at what his hand and foot had done seemingly of their own accord, Alex could only watch in horror as the truck lurched forward. The powerful, eight-cylinder engine propelled the vehicle over the sidewalk and up the stairs of the Rye Police Station. The stairs, where a man stood and looked shocked at the sight of the chrome and metallic blue front end of the truck as it raced towards him.

Alex, drunk as he was, tried to hit the brake, but his foot refused to respond, and it was too late. The truck had too much momentum. Unable to close his eyes, Alex watched in dull horror as the grill slammed into the man and threw him backward.

As the truck shuddered to a halt, the airborne man broke through the plate glass of the station's door. He vomited blood in a wide spray which covered everything as he slammed into the next door and broke it as well.

Oh no, Alex thought. *There's no way he could have survived that.*

CHAPTER 48

DAN BROWN HAS A REVELATION

Dan Brown lay on his back in the foyer of the Rye Police Station. He couldn't see anything. He couldn't hear anything.

He could feel hands on him, though. Someone held his neck steady, and someone else took his hand and squeezed it. He tried to respond, but his fingers only fluttered weakly.

He killed me, Dan thought, and he chuckled silently. *Jesus Christ, that drunk Alex Charles has killed me.*

Dan had arrested Alex a dozen times over the years. All for driving under the influence in that Dodge of his.

And they had never put him away.

Not once.

And now, I'm dying.

He coughed, as he tasted blood and felt broken teeth.

Christ, he thought. *All I wanted was a sandwich.*

Just a sandwich. A BLT.

He felt rather than heard the death rattle in his lungs, and he knew what it meant. Just like those around him knew what the sound stood for.

Whoever held his hand, squeezed it harder.

Dan managed to grip it, and he wondered who tried to comfort him. He wanted to thank them, but he couldn't get his mouth to work.

He felt a sharp pinch in his other hand, and he thought it might be an IV.

They're trying to save me, he thought sadly. *They know I'm dying, but they're trying anyway.*

He felt something cold against his chest, and he figured it was medical scissors. Dan had seen hundreds of accidents. Nothing was a surprise.

Except for what was coming next.

Dan had no idea what to expect.

He had been a good Christian. He had tried to be a good man.

Dan tried to move again, and agony raced through his body. He shrieked and the hand which held his, squeezed harder.

Death didn't creep over Dan.

It slammed into him with all of the weight of Alex's Dodge.

CHAPTER 49
BRIAN AND SHANE TRY TO PLAN

"What do you think?" Shane asked.

"About what?" Brian said.

"Who should go in?" Shane said, lighting a cigarette.

The two men sat on a stone wall which wrapped around an old farm. The air smelled sweetly of spring, and the sun was warm. Midday had slipped by, and the afternoon seemed to be in a rush.

"Just you and me," Brian replied after a moment. "I can see the dead, and you can speak Japanese. It'll be dangerous enough with the two of us. I sure as hell don't want to bring Luke or Jim with us."

"Neither do I," Shane agreed. "I've got this gut feeling we should, though."

Brian was silent for a moment, and then he nodded. "You're right. Feels like we need them both."

"Exactly," Shane said.

Brian scratched his head before he said, "We'll have to take extra precautions. Make sure they stay out of harm's way as much as possible. I just really, *really* wish we didn't have to take them."

"Same here," Shane said. "But the feeling's there, right in the pit of my stomach."

"Me too." Brian shook his head and said, "I hate the idea of putting the two of them in possible danger."

"There's no possible about it," Shane said grimly. "Jim's already experienced some of the violence the dead are capable of. The fact that we're going to be putting a blind man and a young teenager turns my stomach. I mean, we need them. And other than the gut feeling I have, I can't really justify it."

"I can," Brian said. "We need as much help as we can get. Even if one is still a child and the other is a blind senior citizen."

"Yeah. So," Shane said, looking at him. "We'll keep them safe."

"Best we can," Brian said, sighing.

"Let's hope it's enough," Shane said softly.

"Yeah. So," Brian said, standing up and stretching. "Want to head back to town?

"Yeah," Shane said. He got off the wall, yawned and then said, "We'll have to talk to Charles, won't we?"

Brian nodded. "Do you think he has anything big enough to transport multiple skulls at once?"

Shane shrugged. "I don't know. I've never asked him or Ellen the specifics about the ghost prison they run."

"Right," Brian said, chuckling. "Yeah. Feels like the less I know, the better."

"Definitely," Shane said with a grin.

The two of them began the walk back to the center of Rye. As they did so, Brian took a cigar out, lit it, and smoked happily as they went.

"It's nice up here," Shane said shortly.

"It is," Brian agreed. "Too noisy for me now."

"Oh yeah?" Shane asked.

Brian nodded. "Yup. The stress of my job and just the constant strife of life in Manchester drove me crazy. Too much crime. Jenny, my wife, and I, we moved mostly for my sake out to Mont Vernon."

"For the country air?" Shane said, grinning.

"For my heart," Brian said. "Had a couple of heart attacks. Pretty sure the next one will do me in."

Shane looked at him. "You're serious."

"Yup."

"Damn," Shane said. "I'm sorry to hear about that."

Brian shrugged. "Not a whole lot I can do. I take my medicine. But not much more. I mean I don't eat the way I should, and there's no way in hell I'm giving up my whiskey."

"Yeah," Shane said. "Lack of whiskey would be a deal breaker for me, too."

Brian's phone rang, and he pulled it out of his pocket.

The number was one he didn't recognize, but he answered it.

"Hello?" he asked.

"Brian," a young voice said, "this is Jim Bogue."

"Oh, hey Jim, what's going on?" Brian asked, stopping. Shane did as well.

"My grandpa asked if you would be able to come to our house at four, this afternoon. Detective Brown is going to meet us as well," Jim said. "He doesn't want anyone to listen in on our talk about the ghosts."

"Fair enough," Brian said. "What's your address?"

"Fourteen Elwood Street," Jim said, "we're right across from the Church at an angle. It's a Victorian."

"Fourteen Elwood," Brian repeated. "Got it, kid. We'll see you then."

"Okay. Thanks."

Brian ended the call and put the phone away.

"Meeting of the minds?" Shane asked.

"Yeah," Brian said, starting towards downtown again. "I'm assuming the detective found something out. He wants to meet at four at Luke's house."

"Sounds good," Shane said. "Who knows who'll be listening at the coffee shop. Or anywhere else."

"Yup." Brian sighed, tapped the head of ash off his cigar into the street and asked, "So, how do you think we should handle this?"

"Get in touch with Charles first," Shane said. "We'll need whatever containment system he has before we go into the house on Indian Rock Road."

"I was thinking the same thing," Brian said. "If the police do have the Church sealed off, everything will be a little easier. We won't have to worry about anyone getting hurt there."

"And by taking on the house and whoever has the damned skulls, we can make sure no others get transported to the damned place," Shane added.

"Exactly," Brian said, nodding his head.

"Alright," Shane said, grinning around his cigarette, "let's give old Charles a call and see what he has to say."

CHAPTER 50

THE MEETING

Lisa had gone home after the police had questioned them both. Jim knew neither of them were suspects, but it was still uncomfortable to talk to the police. And the officers had seemed on edge.

When Jim had asked his grandfather about it, he had answered it was because of the condition of the body. It was difficult to see a man butchered, even for the police.

At four in the afternoon, Brian and Shane had rung the bell for the main door, and Jim had hurried down to let them in.

Now, the four of them sat with his grandfather and waited for the arrival of Detective Brown.

Footsteps rang out on the stairs, and Jim saw his grandfather frown.

"It's your mother, Jim," he said. "Let her in, please."

Jim got up and opened the door.

His mother smiled, came in, and looked in surprise at Brian and Shane, both of whom stood up as she entered.

Jim introduced them all, and his mother nodded *hello* as the men returned to their seats.

"Wow, Dad," she said, looking around again, a concerned expression on her face. "What's with all of the guests?"

"We're discussing the situation at the Church," Luke said. "These gentlemen have been so kind as to come and assist us."

Jim's mother looked around angrily, as though she had just caught Jim and some of his friends smoking stolen cigarettes.

"What's going on?" his grandfather asked, bringing her attention back to him.

"You remember the detective from the other day?" she asked.

"Detective Brown," his grandfather answered, nodding. "Has he arrived? I asked him to come over."

"No," Jim's mother said, her face becoming pale. "Dad, he's dead."

"What?" his grandfather asked. Then he shook his head. "How?"

"A drunk driver," his mother answered. "The guy's truck jumped the curb, went over the sidewalk and slammed into the detective as he was leaving the Station."

"Oh Jesus," Brian said, sighing.

Shane nodded, and Jim went and sat down, shocked.

"I just wanted to let you know," she said. "I thought it was strange since the officer died of a heart attack in the Church."

"It is strange," his grandfather murmured. "Thank you for telling me, my dear."

"Sure," she said, and she closed the door as she left the room.

"Damn," Brian said. "Damn."

Jim could only nod his agreement.

"Well," his grandfather said, clearing his throat. "I know the detective found out George Montgomery's house at Indian Rock Road is now occupied, and by a man named Miles Cunningham. Dan was going to check if the man had a record, but obviously, we'll never know, now."

Shane rubbed the back of his head and said, "Alright. Brian and I called a colleague of ours down in Nashua. The man and his wife specialize in containing difficult ghosts. We had to leave a message, but basically, we shouldn't make any sort of move until we know we can securely hold the skulls without the ghosts killing us for our trouble."

"Okay," Brian said. "We need to figure out how to get into the Church so we can deal with the situation in there."

"What about one of us, or even all of us, sneaking in?" Jim said tentatively.

"What do you mean, James?" his grandfather asked.

"Someone's snuck in and put the skulls in the Church, right?" Jim asked.

All three of the men nodded.

"So, we should be able to sneak in, too," Jim continued. "I mean, the guy's pretty comfortable getting into the Church, what's to stop him from trying to get in again, or us from doing the same?"

"I think Jim's right," Brian said, nodding. "What is to stop him? He probably went in at night, and I don't think the police are going to put an officer on the place. They'll probably seal everything and return in the morning."

"Which means the guy will have all night," Shane said. He sighed. "Great. So, how do we deal with this situation?"

"Stakeout?" Jim asked.

All of the men laughed, and Jim felt his face go red.

"No, no," Brian said quickly, "we're not laughing at you, Jim. Not at all. It's a good idea."

"Stakeout," his grandfather said gently, "is a term we don't often hear outside of a police drama."

Jim nodded, grinned, and said, "Yeah. I guess I did kind of sound like a TV cop, didn't I?"

"You did, kid," Shane said, chuckling. "But you're right. We should watch the place. I don't know if the guy will come back anytime soon, but he sure does seem to like putting the skulls there."

"Shall we set up a schedule, then?" his grandfather asked.

Brian and Shane looked at him, surprised.

Jim's grandfather smiled. "Just because I cannot see, gentlemen, doesn't mean I can't hear. I'll be able to sit and listen. I do it very well."

"I'm sure you do," Brian said. "Alright, we need a schedule. Is it just between the three of us, or is Jim going to help?"

Jim felt a rush of pride.

"He'll be able to help," his grandfather said. "I would prefer if we did the watching in pairs, however. Jim and I could take the first four hours after sunset. I doubt our ghost transporting friend will make an effort to sneak in while the sun is still up."

"True," Shane said.

Suddenly, Shane's phone rang, and he took it out of his pocket.

"It's Charles," Shane said. "Excuse me, please."

He stepped out of the room as he answered the call.

They waited in silence for a few minutes, until Shane returned.

The man grinned at all of them as he said, "Charles has something. He just has to wait until his wife gets home. He said it was too big for him to move by himself. He'll give us a call when they're on their way."

"Excellent," his grandfather said. "Jim, would you mind putting some water on for coffee, please?"

"Sure," Jim said, and he left the room wondering who Charles was, and what he might be bringing to Rye.

CHAPTER 51

BRIAN HAS A CHAT

Brian was exhausted, and he missed Jenny terribly. He picked at the remnants of a less than satisfactory cheeseburger and wondered how long Charles and Ellen would take.

"Brian."

Brian nearly fell out of his chair at the sound of Leo's voice.

The dead man stood by the hotel room's door, and he looked at Brian with some concern.

"You know your heart is bad?" Leo asked.

"Yes," Brian said, nodding. "I'm aware of that, Leo. Thank you. Did you know scaring the hell out of me doesn't help its condition?"

"Yes," Leo said seriously. "I am, however, far more concerned with the additional stress put on your heart by the level of beef you are eating. I have observed your intake of whiskey as well."

Brian frowned. "Leo, have you been spying on me?"

Leo cleared his throat. "No. I have been watching you. Spying implies I would be gathering information to use against you."

Brian held up a hand, and Leo stopped. "Never mind, Leo. Never mind. Why have you stopped by?"

"Do you know Detective Daniel Brown died this afternoon?" Leo asked.

"Yes," Brian said. He picked up a soggy french fry, tore it in two and popped one-half into his mouth.

"Did you know he was researching the man who now lives in the house on Indian Rock Road?" Leo asked.

Brian nodded.

"Good," Leo said with a smile. "Then he must have told you Miles

Cunningham is a murderer who was recently released from prison."

Brian almost spit the french fry out in surprise. "No, Leo. No, he did not tell us. He died before he could."

"Oh," Leo said. He frowned, and then he smiled. "Ah, I had forgotten. I spoke with him shortly after he died. He was upset he had *not* been able to inform you about the homicidal past of Miles Cunningham."

"You know, Leo," Brian said, sighing. "There is a really, *really* big difference between those two things."

"Yes," Leo agreed. "There is."

Brian shook his head. "Okay, so this guy Cunningham who lives in Montgomery's house, he's a murderer. Who did he kill, and how did he do it?"

"He killed a Catholic Priest," Leo said. "And he strangled him to death."

"Alright," Brian said. "Now, how old was Cunningham when he committed the murder?"

"Eighteen," Leo answered. "There is more, however."

"Tell me 'the more,' Leo," Brian said, eating another fry.

"Miles Cunningham accused the priest of sexual misconduct," Leo said.

"Did they refuse to prosecute the priest?" Brian asked.

"For what?" Leo asked.

"Sexual misconduct," Brian said.

Leo shook his head. "The priest was a genetic eunuch. In addition to this, he had never spent any time alone with Miles Cunningham."

"Oh," Brian said. "What else?"

"The parents of Miles Cunningham were Protestant missionaries in Japan. He speaks the language fluently, and he is quite familiar with the customs," Leo said.

"If his parents were Protestant missionaries," Brian said, "then what was he doing in a Catholic Church?"

"Murdering the priest," Leo answered.

Brian repressed a frustrated sigh. "Okay, Leo, okay. But why did he accuse the priest in the first place?"

"He saw the priest looking at him in a bookstore. He believed the priest sexually assaulted him with his mind," Leo said.

"Jesus," Brian murmured.

"You should be extremely careful, Brian," Leo said. "He was rather brutal in the way he killed the priest."

"Strangulation is brutal any way you look at it, Leo," Brian said.

Leo nodded. "Yes, but Miles Cunningham strangled the priest to death with the man's own intestines."

"His intestines?" Brian asked, after a moment.

"Yes," Leo said. "The police report, which Detective Daniel Brown told me about, stated Miles Cunningham managed to extract six feet of the lower intestine."

"Leo," Brian said, interrupting the dead man.

"Yes, Brian?" Leo asked politely.

"Please, please do not tell me any more about the death of the priest," he said.

Leo nodded. "I shall not."

"Thank you. Does he still have three of the skulls in the house with him?" Brian asked.

"I believe so," Leo said. "But I am sure he will bring another skull to the Church tonight."

"Why?" Brian asked.

"Miles Cunningham converted to Shintoism when he was a young man in Japan. He believes the ghosts are Gods. The only fitting place for a God is in a temple, or a Church," Leo said. "Since he was raised Protestant, Miles feels a Protestant Church is the best place for them."

"Leo," Brian said, shaking his head, "how can you possibly know that?"

"I spoke with Miles this morning," Leo said. "I asked him why he was putting the skulls in the Church. And he explained his reasoning to me. It is unfortunate he is homicidal and delusional, Brian. Miles Cunningham is an extremely intelligent man."

"Great," Brian muttered. "Just great. Leo, did you tell him we were looking for him?"

"No," Leo said, looking confused. "Would you like me to? To be honest, Brian, I thought if I told him what you were planning, it would not work out well."

"No, please, God, no. Leo, just don't communicate with him again, okay?" Brian asked.

"Of course, Brian," Leo said, smiling. "Brian, may I ask you a question?"

"Sure, Leo, shoot," Brian said, and instantly regretted his word choice.

Leo frowned. "Shoot what?"

"No, Leo, go ahead and ask me your question," Brian said, forcing himself to smile.

"I was curious, how is Jenny doing?" Leo asked.

"She's great," Brian said, bemused. "Why do you ask?"

"Sylvia was wondering," Leo said. "She will be glad to hear Jenny is well. In fact, I will tell her now."

Leo vanished.

Brian was alone in his hotel room with half a fifth of Jameson's, limp fries, and a new concern.

Miles Cunningham is crazy, Brian thought. He poured himself a drink, enjoyed a little of it and shook his head. *I don't know which is worse. The murderous ghosts, or a murderous man.*

Guess I'll find out.

He knocked back the whiskey and poured himself another.

CHAPTER 52

THE HURLINGTON HOUSE GETS LOUD

Vic Brooke had lived in flophouses for most of his adult life. He liked to drink more than he liked to work. Hell, he liked just about anything more than work.

At seventy-six years of age, Vic had spent sixty of them in and out of various single men's homes from the Florida Panhandle to Nova Scotia. And after six decades, he knew how to ignore what he heard.

Life was just easier and happier when you minded your own business.

Vic's room was the center of his world. He had two pairs of pants, three pairs of new socks, three pairs of underwear, two tee shirts and one comfortable sweater. He even had a pair of new boots. All of them were courtesy of the kind sisters who ran the Gray Nuns Thrift Shop on Eleventh Street.

Vic always kept his room locked, especially when he was in it. He didn't have much, but people stole just about anything. Vic had done the same himself when he was depressed, and he had been that way more than a few times.

As the evening sun slipped behind the pines of 'Mirkwood', Vic reached up from his narrow bunk and turned on his small lamp. He took a sip of Popov vodka and enjoyed the warmth of the room.

Dry clothes, clean sheets, a bottle of vodka, and some privacy were the little things he treasured.

A glass broke in the hall, and the Swede swore loudly.

The man was a clumsy drunk, and an angry one, too. The whole reason why Vic didn't drink with him anymore.

Vic closed his eyes and enjoyed the pleasant sensation of the vodka as it worked its way into his system.

Glass shattered at the end of the hall and Vic's eyes snapped open.

Sounded like the bathroom mirror, he thought with a sigh. *Old Hurlington said he wasn't going to replace it if we broke it again.*

Vic didn't use the mirror much, not unless he had a problem with one of the few teeth left in his mouth. The reason they couldn't have nice things, though, was because people like the Swede broke them.

The Swede let out a scream and Vic sat up.

The man yelled furiously in Swedish. Someone laughed, and the Swede went silent.

Something heavy dropped in the hallway and the whole floor shook.

More voices rose up, and Vic heard doors open. Someone screamed, another yelled, and he heard dozens of feet pound past his room towards the stairs.

No fire, Vic thought. *The alarm's not going off, and Hurlington makes sure they work. Old man doesn't want to get sued.*

Vic took a nip of the vodka to steady his nerves and looked at his door.

He didn't smell any smoke, and within seconds the hallway was quiet. Not a single sound to be heard.

After another quick drink, Vic put the bottle back on the floor and stretched out again.

Just as he closed his eyes more, noises broke into his silence.

These came from below, on the second floor.

Screams.

Yet these didn't end. They got louder. Worse.

A resident, Vic couldn't quite make out who was begging whom to stop.

Laughter answered the pleas.

The screams grew hoarse.

What's going on? Vic asked himself.

He got off the bed and peeked out the window. On the street in front of the house, he saw most of the other residents. They stood in a rough circle, each face focused on the house. One of them saw him, pointed, and all the others looked as well.

160

Vic saw Bobby Malone, who jumped up and down and waved his arms.

Vic raised his shade, opened his window and leaned forward slightly.

"Get out of the house!" Bobby yelled, desperation and fear in his voice. "Oh for Christ's sake, Vic, get the hell out of there!"

The gathered men took up the cry and beckoned to him.

"Go out the window and onto the roof, Vic!" Bobby called up.

"Christ, Bobby!" Vic yelled. "I'm seventy-six, are you out of your damned mind?"

Before Bobby could answer the doorknob to Vic's room rattled.

Vic backed out of the window and turned around.

The door was locked, as always, and he shook his head. He started to go back to the window, but he stopped as the wood of the frame groaned.

Something heavy tried to get in.

The cheap lock broke, and the door sprang open.

A headless man stood in the opening. He wore a uniform, and he was filthy.

Vic could smell death on the man as he took a step into the room.

In one tan hand, the dead man held a pistol which looked like a Luger, the barrel of which pointed at Vic.

"What the hell?" Vic asked.

Flame erupted from the pistol's mouth, and Vic crumpled over and staggered backward. A terrible, brutally cold fist had slammed into his stomach and knocked the wind out of him.

The pistol barked again, and Vic spun slightly to the right. His leg caught the wall, his hip the window ledge. A third shot punched him in the chest and knocked him through the window.

The sound of breaking glass and laughter chased Vic onto the porch roof. He felt his heart stutter and fail as he rolled across the rough asphalt. He closed his eyes against the world as it spun.

And then Vic was falling.

He didn't care, though. His heart had stopped. Cold spread through his limbs, and he knew he was dying.

He just didn't know how.

Vic slammed into the ground, and thought, *it wasn't even the drink that's done me in.*

CHAPTER 53
MILES CUNNINGHAM THINKS ABOUT THE FUTURE

Miles felt bad about the Reverend.

His parents, if they had still been alive, would have been extremely upset with him. Luckily, however, both of them had passed away in Japan when the tsunami hit.

Well, here's hoping it was lucky, Miles thought. More than likely, both of them had been right with God, but then again, there was always the off chance they weren't.

Miles walked into the kitchen, turned on the faucet and stuck his head into the sink. He took a long drink of the cold water, grinned, and then straightened up. The sunset was nearly finished, and soon he would be able to get the fourth skull over to the Church.

And once the Japanese are gone, he thought, wiping his mouth dry with his sleeve, *I'll be able to finish up with the other ghosts.*

He wandered into the den, sat down on the floor and dragged his blanket over to him. He thought about the curious ghost who had visited him earlier, and wondered if he would see him again.

Either way, the conversation had been extremely interesting.

The ghost had questioned Miles extensively about the dead Japanese soldiers. He had asked why Miles moved them, and how he did it as well. And he was extremely polite.

Miles smiled.

He liked polite people. Especially polite dead people.

The Japanese men were not polite. They treated him as though he were inferior, which, he knew, he was.

But that's beside the point, Miles told himself.

Leo was polite.

And Miles smiled again.

Leo had also brought up several good points, the most important one being what if the Japanese decided to kill him when they were all together again.

Miles had worried about the same.

The Japanese men were none too pleased with their move. Yes, he had given them all plenty of saké, but it only made them drunk.

Not forgetful.

They had been happy in George's house. Perfectly happy to be in the fallout shelter with all of the other ghosts.

Miles hadn't been happy, though. Especially when they had threatened to kill him.

It would only have been a matter of time before one of them did.

They liked blood a little too much.

And so Leo had posed a valid question.

How was Miles going to get away?

He hadn't committed any crime, except illegally entering the Church, so he didn't have to worry too much about the police. Although fear still nagged at him about any trace evidence left behind at the murder scenes.

No, the real worry was how to live after he delivered the last ghost.

I should bring Ichiru last, Miles realized. *He'll be able to talk them out of killing me. Yes. He's the most rational of them.*

He let out a long sigh and nodded to himself, happy with the solution he had discovered.

He turned out the light and snuggled down into the warmth of the blanket. He could faintly smell death, but he wasn't certain whether it was the house or the dead in the fallout shelter.

It doesn't matter, he thought. *You need to get some sleep. You have another trip to make.*

With a smile on his lips, Miles closed his eyes and waited for his dreams.

CHAPTER 54

MEETING WITH THE GOTTESMANS

Brian and Shane stood in the parking lot of the hotel. They had the gate of Shane's pickup down, and they waited in silence. Charles and Ellen were due to arrive at any moment, and they would have the containment unit with them.

Brian didn't know what it was. Neither did Shane.

It'll work, Brian told himself. *They have done it before. They can do it again.*

Several minutes passed and then an older model, blue Ford truck appeared.

"There they are," Shane said, straightening up.

Brian did the same and waved.

The truck's lights flashed, and it pulled into the space beside Shane's truck.

Ellen got out of the driver's seat and smiled tightly at both of them. She looked from Shane to Brian and asked, "Do I even want to know what it is you two have in the works here?"

"I doubt it," Shane said.

"I've been telling her the same thing the whole way up," Charles said, closing the passenger side door. "Come on 'round the back."

Brian and Shane walked over and waited as Ellen and Charles released several tie downs which kept a blue, plastic tarp in place. A moment later, Charles pulled the sheet aside and folded it.

Revealed was a large wooden crate, almost the size of an old, military footlocker.

"This," Charles said, "is heavy as hell."

"It's lined with lead," Ellen added. "Which is why Hercules here needed me to help him carry it."

Charles grinned.

"So," Ellen said, looking at Brian and Shane. "What are you two doing with this, tonight?"

"Tonight," Brian said, "we're going to try and put three skulls into it."

Ellen looked over at Charles, and asked, "Whose?"

"We don't know yet," Shane said. "We just know we have half a dozen angry, dead Japanese soldiers, and we need to contain them."

"How angry?" Ellen asked.

"Four dead, two maimed, and one hurt," Brian answered.

"Oh my," Ellen muttered.

Charles looked at Brian. "Boy, you sure know how to pick 'em, Champ."

"Yeah," Brian said, sighing.

"Does Jenny know how bad this is?" Ellen asked.

Brian nodded.

"And what about you?" Ellen said, turning to face Shane.

"Me?" he asked in surprise.

"Yes, you," Ellen said. "What brings you out of Nashua? Usually, you don't go anywhere."

"The dead speak Japanese," Shane said.

"And Brian called you?" Ellen asked. Before Shane could answer she turned to Charles. "No. Charles called you."

Charles cleared his throat nervously.

Ellen shook her head and remained quiet.

"Anyway," Charles said a moment later. He gave the box a pat. "You'll need to have this with you when you grab the skulls. I also included a pair of white cotton gloves for each of you. If these skulls are as bad as you say, then you're going to want to have the gloves on."

"What for?" Brian asked.

"Some objects," Charles said, "have this negative effect when there's direct contact between them and flesh. This may not be the case with the skulls, but, as I'm sure you'll agree, it's much, much better to be safe than sorry."

Brian nodded.

"Does the box lock?" Shane asked.

Charles nodded. "I'll give you the key in a minute. Just listen first, please. You make sure this box is open, and as soon as you have the skulls, you put them in and close the damned lid. And you *lock it*. Understood?"

Brian and Shane nodded.

"Good," Charles said. He pulled a key out of his pocket and handed it to Shane.

"Now, Charles," Brian said, "what do we do about the second batch of skulls?"

Charles frowned.

"What second batch?" Ellen asked.

"Well, the six skulls are separated into two groups of three," Brian said. "What do we do when we have to put the second group in?"

"I will help."

The four of them jumped as Leo appeared by Brian.

"Did I frighten you?" Leo asked.

Ellen shook her head angrily and got back into the truck. She slammed the door closed, started the engine and turned on the radio.

"The answer to your question, Leo," Brian said as gently as possible, "would be 'yes,' you did scare us."

"I am sorry," Leo said sincerely. "I did not mean to frighten you."

"It's okay. You're going to help them?" Charles asked.

"Yes, I am going to help them," Leo replied.

"How?" Shane asked.

Leo looked at him and said, "When the time comes, I will make sure the three ghosts go into the box."

Shane looked as though he wanted to ask more, but he didn't.

"However," Leo said, "you are going to want to do all of this soon."

"Why?" Brian asked. "What's happened, Leo?"

"The First Church purchased the Hurlington House property," Leo said.

Shane frowned. "Why is that important?"

"Since the Church owns the property now," Leo said, "the boundaries of the Church have expanded."

"Oh," Brian said softly.

Shane sighed.

"Has anyone else been hurt?" Brian asked.

"Yes," Leo answered.

"How many?" Brian said.

"There are two on the first floor, one on the second, and one on the third. There is also another on the lawn," Leo replied.

"And they're all hurt?" Shane asked.

Leo shook his head. "They are all dead. The one on the lawn was the last, and I am most curious about his death. They fired something at him, almost a spectral bullet. This is extremely interesting, Brian."

"Leo," Brian said, "please, we don't need any details."

"Oh," Leo said. He looked closely at Brian. "I see you are upset about this."

"Yes, Leo," Brian said. "I am upset about this."

"When you are dead you will not be upset," Leo said confidently. "You will understand death, and therefore, it will hold no mystery for you. And without mystery, you will be without fear."

"Fantastic, Leo, fantastic," Brian said, sighing. "Listen, I'm not dead, so I am upset, and let's leave it there, okay?"

"Okay," Leo agreed, smiling.

"Leo," Shane said.

"Yes, Shane?" Leo asked.

"Should we get the ghosts in the house on Indian Rock Road first?" Shane asked.

"Yes," Leo answered.

"Any particular reason why?" Brian asked.

"Yes," Leo said.

Brian waited a moment, and when Leo didn't answer, Brian said, "And what is the reason, Leo?"

"Ah, yes," Leo said, grinning. "The reason. It is simple. Miles Cunningham has already left his house with the fourth skull. He is making his way to the Church now. The house is unprotected by him."

"Excellent," Shane said. "Let's get the box into my truck, and then we can pick up Luke and Jim. Charles?"

Charles nodded and the two men started to drag the heavy box out.

"Shane," Brian said hesitantly, "I really feel bad about bringing Luke and his grandson."

"You have to," Leo said before Shane could answer.

Charles and Shane managed to get the box onto the bed of the truck.

"Who are Luke and Jim?" Charles asked, wiping the sweat off his brow.

"A blind man and his teenage grandson," Shane answered.

"Jesus," Charles said, looking at Brian. "Yeah, I can see why you feel bad about it, Brian."

"Why do we have to?" Brian asked Leo.

"The dead will remember Luke," Leo said. "They will see his eyes. They will understand him. They might even listen to him. But you must bring Luke, and Jim, and saké."

"Why saké?" Charles asked, looking confused.

"Because they do not like to travel sober," Leo said.

"Hold on," Shane said. "How the hell do ghosts get drunk?"

"They drink," Leo said, and he vanished.

"Him disappearing," Shane said, looking over at Brian, "is annoying the hell out of me."

Brian shook his head and chuckled. "Pretty sure it's only going to get worse, my friend."

CHAPTER 55
LUKE, MR. BOYD, AUGUST 15, 1967

"You look good, Luke," Mr. Boyd said. "You look good."

The two of them sat on the older man's porch and in spite of the August heat, Luke wore his blue uniform.

"You spending all of your leave here?" Mr. Boyd asked.

"Yes," Luke said, and then he grinned, "it's about all I can afford as a second lieutenant."

Mr. Boyd chuckled and nodded his head. "I won't even tell you what they paid me as a Private when I enlisted, boy. Don't worry, though, you'll figure out how to make it stretch. Want a beer?"

"Please," Luke said.

Mr. Boyd reached down into his cooler, pulled out a pair of bottles, popped the tops off and handed one to Luke.

The beer was cold and strong, and Luke smiled. "Thanks."

"You're welcome," Mr. Boyd said. He drank some of his and after a minute he said, "You know it's going to be hard?"

Luke nodded.

"We can tell you what to expect," Mr. Boyd said. "How it's going to sound and feel. But no one, no one can tell you how you're going to react to combat. Some men break. Some men love it. Some men deal with it and put it behind them. Men you thought would lead the way, they'll shrink back and run. Others, the little guy you never thought would be able to keep up on a march, hell, I've seen 'em turn into gods of death."

Mr. Boyd shook his head. He looked at his beer, and then he smiled.

"Just be true to your Marines, Luke," Mr. Boyd said. "Let everything else fall by the road."

"Yes, sir," Luke said.

"Come on," Mr. Boyd said, standing up suddenly. "I've got a going away party for you."

Luke got to his feet and asked, "What party?"

Mr. Boyd chuckled and shook his head. "Come on, come on. Let's not ruin the surprise."

Luke followed him into the house and to the war room. Mr. Boyd unlocked the door and led the way in.

Even with Mrs. Boyd absent from the home, Mr. Boyd closed and locked the door behind him. Luke noticed several large bottles of saké by the skulls, as well as a bottle of Black Label whiskey.

Luke looked over at Mr. Boyd.

The man smiled. "They wanted to say goodbye as well."

The air shimmered slightly, and the dead Japanese men appeared. They looked younger, their uniforms fresh.

"They appreciate a man who goes to war," Mr. Boyd said. "They appreciate the warrior spirit."

One of the ghosts spoke in Japanese, and Mr. Boyd nodded before he turned to Luke and translated.

"Ichiru wishes for you to have a safe journey to your war. He knows you will fight with honor," Mr. Boyd said.

One of the other men added a few words.

Mr. Boyd chuckled. "And Sato, Sato hopes you'll die well."

Luke laughed, bowed and said, "Please tell them I said thank you."

Mr. Boyd did so, and he poured the saké.

CHAPTER 56

TRAVELING

Luke sat in the front passenger seat of Brian's car and listened to the various sounds of the engine. In his hands, he held a bottle of whiskey and wondered if the Japanese soldiers would accept the gift. Someone, and Luke suspected it was Miles, had bought out the local supply of saké.

Again, he thought of the dead Japanese soldiers.

He remembered them. He recalled the drinks they had together, and the stories the men had shared with him. Horrific tales of war, first in China, and then on islands in the Pacific.

In his mind's eye, Luke could picture them perfectly.

Will they remember me? Luke wondered, shifting his hands on the bottle of Black Label. *Will they care if they do?*

A flutter of fear passed through his stomach, and he coughed nervously.

"Are you okay, Luke?" Brian asked.

"Yes," Luke replied. "Just a little nervous."

"Understandable," Brian said.

"I don't like my grandson being here," Luke said.

"I know," Brian said. "I don't like him being here, either. I'd rather he was at home, safe."

"It's alright," Jim said. "I'm the only one who can help my grandfather get around places he doesn't know. He doesn't trust anyone else. You and Shane have to deal with the ghosts, right?"

"Right," Brian said, sighing.

"James," Luke said.

"Yes, sir?" James asked.

"Let's go over this again, alright?" Luke said.

"Yes," James said with a grumble.

Brian chuckled.

"James," Luke said, "where will you be the entire time we are in the house?"

"By your side, holding onto your arm," James said, wisely keeping his voice neutral.

"And what will you do if I tell you to run, James?" Luke asked.

"I will run, sir," James answered.

"Basically, what are you supposed to do, James?" Luke said.

"Whatever you say, Grandpa."

"Why?"

"Because it's dangerous."

"Extremely so," Luke said.

"Remember what the ghosts did to you at the Church," Brian said. "And remember what you saw in the graveyard, okay?"

"I will," James said in a low voice. "I will."

Luke shifted the bottle of whiskey in his hands, felt the cool glass beneath his fingers, and once more he wondered what they would find in the house.

CHAPTER 57
TEN INDIAN ROCK ROAD

Shane had been watching the house for half an hour, and no one was in it. A Camry had been parked in the driveway when he first passed by an hour prior, but it was gone.

He hadn't seen any ghosts either, but then again he could only see a couple of windows.

Miles Cunningham, the man with the skulls, had left.

Probably with another ghost.

Shane sighed and glanced into the back of the truck. The trunk the Gottesmans had dropped off was there. On his lap, he had a pair of white, cotton gloves. Brian had the other pair. Shane had already unlocked the container and made sure it could be opened easily.

He swallowed nervously and felt sweat build up at the base of his skull.

Shane knew what the dead were capable of. He knew what these particular ghosts were capable of.

And none of it, absolutely *none of it*, was good.

The sound of an engine caught Shane's attention, and he turned towards it. A moment later, Brian's car came around the corner and pulled up behind Shane's pickup.

Brian, Jim, and Luke got out of the car. The blind man held a bottle of Black Label whiskey.

"Damn, Luke," Shane said, grinning, "you must like your whiskey."

Luke smiled. "Love my whiskey. Breaks my heart having to share it with the dead."

The men chuckled, and Jim smiled.

"Well," Brian said, "this is going to be interesting. We'll have to go into the house and pretty much stay together. Shane and I will be carrying the box. Jim, you'll obviously be leading your grandfather. Luke, just don't drop the whiskey."

"I won't," Luke said.

"Since we're looking for a fallout shelter," Brian continued, "we'll be going down into the basement. Shane and I will go first. If anything happens, I'd rather it be to us."

Shane nodded in agreement. "Let's make sure nothing does happen."

"My grandpa already went through what I need to do," Jim said.

"And what's that?" Shane asked.

"Whatever he tells me to," Jim answered.

The men shared another chuckle.

Shane turned to Brian. "Ready?"

"Not at all," Brian said. "But let's get it done."

Together they pulled the box out of the trunk, and it was heavy.

"For as much as this weighs," Shane said, feeling sweat form under his arms and along his spine, "this damned thing better work."

"It will," Brian said. "But it definitely isn't good for my heart."

"Hey," Shane said, "I'm not giving any mouth to mouth if you keel over. Just letting you know."

"Fair enough," Brian said with a chuckle. "Fair enough."

Shane took the lead and crossed the street. Indian Rock Road was sparsely inhabited, and he hadn't seen any traffic while he had waited. A few houses were further up, but nothing close to number ten.

Small blessings, he thought.

When they reached the side steps, he and Brian put the box down.

"Don't suppose you know how to pick a lock, do you?" Brian asked.

"I do," Shane said. He climbed the steps, opened the screen door, held it in one hand, and kicked.

His boot landed solidly just at the deadbolt with enough force to rip the lock free of the frame. The wood screamed in protest, and the door whipped in and ricocheted off the interior wall.

"I said 'pick'," Brian said with a smile.

"Oh," Shane said, grinning. "My bad. I thought you said 'kick.'"

"Well," Brian said, "that works, too."

"I'll check it out," Shane said. "Be right back."

Shane left them on the side steps and entered the house. He flicked on the light and looked around. The place was in the process of being repaired, and whoever Miles Cunningham was, he was a good handyman. The floor was torn up, but the subfloor had been leveled. The drywall was bare of paint, but it looked as though it had been mudded properly.

Too bad he's crazy, Shane thought.

Shane went directly to a pair of doors, one across from the other, just on the other side of the kitchen.

The first door opened to a bathroom. The second led down into the basement.

Jackpot, Shane thought. He turned on the basement light. In spite of how carefully he walked, each stair squeaked loudly. When he reached the cement floor, he saw the basement was empty. A few bare bulbs were suspended from the ceiling and a water heater stood off to one corner. Beside it was a cheap, pressboard door.

Shane walked to it, opened the door and looked into the furnace room.

Now, if I were a paranoid man, living in the atomic era, where would I hide my end of the world bunker? Shane asked himself. *Behind the furnace, of course.*

He went to the old machine, peered around the aged metal and caught sight of an open doorway.

Beyond it was a room full of shelves, most of which were empty. But Shane did see some militaria, and he knew he was in the right place.

Shane quickly slipped back up the stairs and to the others.

"Did you find it?" Brian asked.

"I did," Shane said. "Behind the furnace in the basement. We'll have to bring the box all the way down as close as we can."

Brian nodded. "Luke?"

"Yes?" he asked.

"When we get down there, we may or may not have the ghosts greet us. If we do, I think our best bet is for you to hold up the whiskey and tell them your name," Brian said.

"You don't sound especially confident," Luke said.

"Probably because I'm not," Brian said. "We're going to need Jim down there, just off to one side. We can't leave him up here because we need to carry the damned box and he needs to help you."

"I'll be okay," Jim said in a small voice.

Shane looked at the boy and remembered his own fear as a child.

"I know you will," Shane said after a moment. "Just listen and do as you're told."

"I will," Jim said.

"Ready, Brian?" Shane asked.

"Yup. Gloves?" Brian asked.

"Might as well," Shane said. He and Brian took the white gloves out, put them on, and then they picked up the chest again.

Wordlessly, they brought it into the house, navigated the stairs, and managed to get the container into the furnace room. Luke, with Jim's assistance, followed them and soon all four stood together.

"Alright," Brian said. "Let's do this. Luke, Jim, stay here. If we yell, Luke, offer it up."

"I will," Luke replied. "Jim, stand by the door, please."

"To the shelter?" Jim asked.

Luke smiled. "No, my dear boy, by the one we entered."

Shane looked over to Brian and asked, "Are you ready?"

The man nodded and the two of them went into the fallout shelter.

Brian looked around, let out a surprised laugh and took an item off one of the shelves.

"What?" Shane asked, glancing over at Brian.

"Here, catch," Brian said, and he tossed the item to Shane, who caught it easily.

It was a pair of brass knuckles, except they were made out of what looked and felt like iron. They had sharpened points hammered into the metal. "What the hell were these used for?"

"Trench warfare," Brian answered. "Looks like they're made out of iron though. Keep 'em. They'll come in handy."

"How do you figure?" Shane asked. "You can't actually punch a ghost."

"You can with iron," Brian said. He held up his right hand and wiggled the index finger. There was a wide iron ring on it. "Trust me. Just put them on."

Shane shrugged, slid the iron knuckle-dusters on over his glove, and turned his attention to the skulls.

CHAPTER 58

THE CONTEST BEGINS

Luke could hear the fearful, labored breath of James. The heavy, nervous tread of Shane and Brian as they entered the fallout shelter.

Luke stood in his darkness and held onto the bottle of whiskey. He shifted his grip, conscious of the sweat on his palms.

"There," Shane said.

And suddenly a horrific scream erupted.

The two men yelled in surprise and anger. Shane yelled out in Japanese, and it was answered in kind, and furiously. With a deep breath, Luke added his own, raised voice to the cacophony.

"I am Lieutenant Luke James Allen," he said, pitching his voice deeply, the words slamming into the concrete walls. "I bring a gift to the men of Imperial Japan."

A coldness wrapped around Luke, and he knew they were there.

The dead surrounded him, pressed close.

Cold fingers touched his eyes, traced the scars they found.

"Marine," one of the dead said. "War."

Luke could only nod and hold up the bottle of whiskey.

The hands fell away from his eyes and Luke breathed a small sigh of relief.

Luke uncorked the bottle of whiskey, took a good, long drink from it, then he wiped the bottle's lip with his sleeve. His hands shook as he held it in front of him. A moment later, a chill swept over him and someone took the bottle from him.

One of the two ghosts laughed and said, "Whiskey."

The other replied in Japanese. There was a pause and then Luke felt the bottle being pressed back into his hands.

"Thank you," he said, and took another drink before holding it out once more.

As the bottle was taken from him a second time, Luke faintly heard Brian speak to Shane.

A single, sharp word was spoken. A second voice snapped a reply Luke could not understand, and then a terrible, icy grip took hold of his heart and squeezed.

CHAPTER 59

JIM SEES TOO MUCH

After his grandfather had yelled out his own name, Jim saw two ghosts appear. They stood on either side of his grandfather, and they reached up and touched his face.

Jim watched, unable to look away as they examined his eyes and spoke to one another softly. He caught the word 'Marine,' but nothing else.

Jim watched as his grandfather opened the whiskey, took a drink of it and held it out. The first ghost took it, drank, and then the second did the same before he gave it to his grandfather again. Once more, his grandfather drank, and then the first Japanese ghost took the bottle of whiskey again.

From the hidden room, Jim heard Brian speak to Shane. One of the Japanese soldier's spoke and the other replied angrily.

The first soldier thrust his hands into his grandfather's chest.

His grandfather gasped, collapsed to his knees and fell slowly to the left. The entire time the ghost kept his hands in his grandfather's chest. He sank down to the floor and never looked away. Something rattled loudly as his grandfather breathed, and then he stopped.

His grandfather lay still on the cement floor as the ghost withdrew his hands and bowed.

The ghost with the whiskey uncapped it, brought the mouth of the bottle to his nose and seemed to smell it.

Brian and Shane hurried out of the room, each with a skull.

The dead turned to face them, but it was too late.

The skulls were dropped into the open box unceremoniously, and the lid slammed closed. The ghosts disappeared, and the bottle crashed to the floor. It shattered and glass shards and drops of whiskey struck Jim, who stood silently by the door.

"Oh, damn," Brian said, hurrying to Jim's grandfather.

Shane locked the box and stepped away as it rattled on the floor. Screams of rage, which sounded like nothing more than the plaintive wails of kittens, slipped free of the confines of the chest.

"He's dead," Jim said. He looked from Shane to Brian. "My grandfather's dead."

Brian nodded.

Jim looked at his grandfather for a long moment.

A sudden, sharp pain exploded in his chest and he let out a long, terrible cry. Tears spilled from his eyes and his body was wracked with sobs. For several long, agonized minutes he fought to control himself, and finally, he did. He snuffled back the tears, took a deep breath and said hoarsely, "We still have four more to catch."

"Yes," Shane agreed softly, looking away. "Yes, we do."

"We can put your grandfather in my car," Brian said, clearing his throat uncomfortably and standing up.

Jim shook his head. "No, we can't. We have to get to the Church. We can come back for my grandfather's body. But we can't wait. We have to stop them before anyone else gets hurt."

Jim walked to his grandfather, to the man who had been everything, and dropped to a knee. He leaned forward, kissed the furrowed brow, and held back more tears. *I'll cry when they're all in the box,* Jim told himself. *I'll cry then.*

CHAPTER 60

THE CHURCH

The three of them entered the Church together through the broken back door.

Leo stood in the late Reverend's office.

"Is he here?" Brian asked.

"Yes," Leo said. "Miles Cunningham is in the basement. By the furnace."

"Creature of habit," Shane murmured, and Brian nodded his agreement. Jim walked to the desk and straightened up spilled pencils and pens.

"Does he have the fourth skull?" Brian asked, afraid the answer would be 'no.'

"He does," Leo said.

The box shook in his grip, and Brian glanced at Shane.

"These gentlemen are not happy," Shane said.

"Why would they be?" Leo asked, confused. "You have locked them in a box."

"Don't worry about it, Leo," Brian said. "Lead on to the furnace, please."

Leo nodded, turned and walked through the door.

Brian sighed, but Jim slipped in front and opened it for them.

"Thanks, kid," Brian said.

Jim nodded and followed them as they caught sight of Leo by another door. This one was not closed, but it had a large 'X' made of yellow police tape over it.

Shane knocked it aside and started down the stairs.

The lights were on, and when they reached the basement, they found Miles Cunningham.

He stood at the far end of the room by a door marked 'Furnace.'

He was a small man. Smaller than Leo had been in life. He was slim as well, and he looked completely and utterly mad. The clothes he wore were old and disheveled. His expression was a mixture of shock and outrage.

"Hi, Miles!" Shane said cheerfully.

Miles blinked and looked confused.

"Do I know you?" he asked.

"Nope!" Shane said. "Where are the skulls?"

"What skulls?" Miles asked sulkily. He took a step to the left, and his eyes flickered towards the stairs.

"No," Shane said. "No, no, no. You can't leave. We need the skulls first. Then you can leave."

Before Miles could answer Leo appeared in the room. "They are here. In a spot beneath a duct. The men are very upset. I do not believe I can keep them back for long."

Miles looked surprised. "You are real!"

"I am," Leo said, and then he vanished again.

"Wait," Miles said, turning back to Brian and Shane. "What are you going to do?"

"We're going to take the skulls," Brian said, nodding to Shane. Together they set the box down. "We're going to take them someplace nice."

"No," Miles said, shaking his head. "No. This is someplace nice. You can't take them anywhere else. I won't let you."

"We're not asking you," Shane said, and he walked towards the furnace room.

Brian followed.

Miles took a step towards them and suddenly Jim was there.

The teenager was a blur as he slammed into Miles' back and knocked him down.

"Quickly!" Leo yelled from the other room.

Brian glanced at Jim to see if the boy needed help, but Miles was on the floor with Jim on top of him. The teenager was pure rage, driving Miles' head repeatedly into the floor.

"Brian," Shane said, wrenching the door to the furnace room open, "he can hold his own for a minute. We need the skulls."

Reluctantly, Brian followed Shane. Screams filled the small space, and Brian felt as though he had walked through a physical barrier of sound. Shane got to the duct first, reached up and found a loose cinder block.

He threw it aside and revealed a small cavity, in which four skulls sat. Without any sort of grace, Shane reached in, grabbed two and tossed them to Brian, who caught them easily. The noise pounded at his head as he staggered out of the room and towards the box. He fell to his knees, vomited from the constant barrage of sound and waited in his own bile for Shane to join him.

Shane did so a moment later. He dropped the skulls to the floor where they rolled across the parquet and stopped against the box. He fumbled for the key, found it, unlocked the chest and fell back as the two ghosts within, barreled out.

The dead rushed at Brian and Shane.

Shane screamed out something in Japanese which caused the ghosts to pause for a heartbeat, but it was enough for Brian to get to his feet.

One of the dead men turned on him, snarling, and Brian shouted as he slammed his right hand into the ghost's head. When the iron ring connected with the dead man, he vanished.

"The skulls!" Brian called out. "Get them into the box, Shane!"

Shane climbed to his hands and knees. As he reached for a skull, one of the other Japanese soldiers tried to stop him and Brian stepped between them. The dead man grabbed Brian's left arm, the grip painfully cold. Stars burst in front of Brian's eyes and for a brief moment he was afraid of another heart attack.

Yet, instead of collapsing, Brian thrust his right hand into the ghost's belly. The dead man vanished.

Before Brian could relish the small victory, the other four men swarmed around him. A cold, hard force pierced his shoulder while something hard slammed into the side of his head. Brian stumbled, tripped over Shane and fell onto his back.

He swung wildly, missed a Japanese soldier and tried to get himself back on his feet.

Shane let out a shriek of pain as one of the dead thrust a hand into his thigh and squeezed. With his face red with agony Shane managed to punch the ghost in the side of his head with the iron knuckle-dusters. The dead man vanished with a howl.

Brian started to push himself up and received a kick in the head for it. The world went black and he felt a tooth pop out of its socket. Blood rushed into his mouth and he gagged on it.

When his vision cleared, he found himself on his side, lying in his own filth again. What he saw, though, was horrifying.

Shane was on his back, pinned to the floor by two of the ghosts. The third, holding a wicked looking knife, stood over him.

And then Leo was there. Leo launched himself forward, his face free of emotion as his left hand became a ball of pure red light. He struck the knife wielding soldier in the back, square between the shoulder blades and the man shuddered. The weapon vanished, the Japanese man screaming as Leo dragged him towards the chest.

One of the other soldiers let go of Shane's right hand to rush to the aid of his comrade, and Shane rolled. The knuckle-dusters glowed dully in the light and Shane smashed the dead man in the face, causing the soldier to disappear.

Leo stood, one hand within a ghost while he faced the last soldier.

"Come, Ichiru," Leo said, nodding to the final ghost. "Come for Sato and let us be done with this."

Ichiru smiled, a broad, foul expression which filled Brian with fear as he looked upon them. His smile spoke of hate and a desire to inflict pain. It was sadistic and it reminded him of the King of Middlebury Sanitarium.

Ichiru raised his hands, palms open to show he was unarmed, and then he attacked.

The dead man was incredibly fast, yet Leo was faster, even with Sato hanging limply from his hand. Leo moved under a pair of quick punches from Ichiru and lashed out with his freehand, catching Ichiru in the chest and sending him stumbling back.

Ichiru laughed coldly, and moved forward again. His next strike, a kick, landed. The whole Church shook as Leo took the full brunt of the blow in his stomach. Brian saw Leo's eyes widen in shock and pain.

"The box, Brian Roy!" Leo yelled, sidestepping a blow from Ichiru while Sato twisted on his hand and tried to reach Leo's arm. "Please, open the box!"

Brian suddenly was beside it, all six of the skulls just inches away. Ignoring the pain pounding through him, Brian snatched up the skulls and threw them into the chest. He didn't wait for Leo to tell him to close it. Instead, he slammed the top down, and locked it.

The noise vanished and Brian collapsed back onto the floor.

"Well done," Leo said, smiling softly. "Well done."

And Leo walked out of the room

"Holy Jesus," Shane whispered.

Brian could only nod. Then, with more strength than he believed he still possessed, he pushed himself up. "Jim!"

He twisted around and saw the teenager.

Jim sat on the floor beside the body of Miles Cunningham.

Jim had a piece of his shirt, and he wiped the handle of a letter opener carefully.

"Suicide is a terrible thing," Jim said softly. The polished brass opener was buried in Miles's chest, just under the sternum.

"Such a terrible thing," Jim repeated. He picked up Miles's right hand and wrapped it around the instrument's handle. Jim looked at Brian.

"Suicide is even worse when it's done in a Church," Jim said.

The teenager stood up, looked from the body to the box and then to Brian and Shane. "I'd like to go get my grandfather now."

The boy left the room.

Brian and Shane watched him go and listened to his footsteps on the stairs.

"Damn," Shane said after a moment.

And Brian could only nod in agreement.

CHAPTER 61
SAYING GOODBYE

Brian stood off to one side of the road which ran through the Veterans' Cemetery in Boscawen, New Hampshire. Jim had invited him and Shane to attend, and they had.

Brian wiped tears out of the corners of his eyes as a bugler finished 'Taps'.

Shane patted Brian on the shoulder, and he saw Shane's eyes welled with tears as well.

"I'll wait in the car," Shane said, clearing his throat and brushing the tears away.

Brian nodded and looked back to the graveside.

There was a decent crowd, as far as funerals went, and Brian waited patiently for his turn to offer his condolences to both Jim and the boy's mother.

'Boy' doesn't quite cut it now, Brian thought.

If anything, Jim was a young man; one who had witnessed his grandfather's death and had his revenge on the man who had set the death into motion.

Mourners passed by and Brian watched as Lisa, hardly recognizable outside of the Riverwalk, gave Jim a not-so-chaste kiss on the lips before she walked away. Finally, when the crowd had thinned and Jim and his mother where relatively alone, Brian approached.

Both the young man's eyes and his mother's were red. She held a folded American flag to her chest and looked down at the silver casket in the grave.

She turned at his approach and offered him a small, weary smile.

"Mr. Roy," she said. "Thank you for coming."

"You're welcome," Brian said.

"I can't thank you enough for helping bring my father to the hospital," she said. "Even if it was too late."

"I'm just sorry I had left them with the car," Brian said, the lie sticking in his throat. "If I had thought your father would have a heart attack, I never would have brought them with me."

She smiled sadly and shook her head. "Please don't worry about it, Mr. Roy. My father loved to talk about the town, and about history. I'm just pleased he was with Jim when he passed."

Jim dropped his chin to his chest and remained silent.

"If you'll excuse me, Mr. Roy," Jim's mother said, "but I have to see the new Reverend about meeting at the Elks Lodge for dinner with the others."

"Of course," Brian said. He stood beside Jim as she hurried away to catch up with the Reverend.

After a moment, Brian asked Jim, "How is he?"

"Who?" Jim asked, looking up, his eyes swollen and bright red.

"The new Reverend," Brian said, nodding towards the man and Jim's mother.

Jim shrugged. "He's no Rev."

"Understood," Brian said. "So, what's next for you?"

"School," Jim said. "Hang out with Lisa and my friends. Maybe get a job. Maybe not. Depends on how much mom is going to need me."

"Well," Brian said. "I think she'll need you a lot. Don't go looking for a job yet."

Jim nodded and then he looked at Brian. "What about you? What are you going to do?"

"What do you mean?" Brian asked.

"I mean, are you still going to do the whole ghost thing?" Jim asked.

"Of course," Brian said with a grin. "It's what I do."

"Really?" Jim said, surprised.

"Really," Brian said. "In fact, when school's out for the summer, give me a call. We can work on some stuff up here, together."

"Yeah?" Jim asked.

"Yeah," Brian said. "You're tough as nails, kid."

"Maybe," Jim said, glancing at his grandfather's casket, "but I'm not as tough as my grandpa."

Brian couldn't argue with him. Luke Allen had been a hell of a man.

Brian looked at the clouds, then at the rows of the dead. Among the stones and well cared for graves, he saw ghosts of old soldiers, sailors and Marines. Men and women who had watched another comrade laid to rest.

With a final glance at Luke's grave, Brian put his hands into his pockets and walked towards his car, ready for the long ride home.

* * *

JANUARY 5TH, 1968

George's face hurt with the cold.

A dull ache radiating from his left orbital socket.

The one the war-lover had broken.

Absently, George, with his tongue, probed at the spot where two of his back teeth had been knocked out. The same punch which had broken the socket had knocked out the teeth.

The war-lover had had big hands.

Hard fists.

Steel-toed boots.

But the war-lover was dead, and his wife as well.

Which meant the hideous trophies the war-lover had kept were unguarded. George could get them and put them away. He could make sure no one ever used the items for the glorification of mass murder again.

The sun finished its early descent behind the ranks of pine trees which lined the war-lover's back yard, and George moved.

His body was stiff. For hours, he had sat still in the cold. Patience was necessary. George needed to make sure no one stopped by to check on the house. Thankfully Luke Allen, the insufferable athlete, had joined the Marines and was off in Vietnam.

With any luck, Allen would die as well.

George couldn't stand any of them.

All of the athletes. All of the war-lovers. All of those who believed in America, 'right or wrong.'

George snorted derisively and stepped out of the tree line. He glanced to the left and to the right, saw the shades drawn in the houses on either side of the war-lover's home, and he quickly moved forward.

He was dressed in white, and he carried a small pry bar which he knew would let him open the back door. Each step was cautious and silent.

George's father, who had passed on already, had taught George to hunt and to take only what he needed from the land.

And George was hunting; he sought the remnants of war.

In a matter of moments, he was at the back door, and he had the pry bar out. With hardly any noise, he slipped the slim metal in, popped the latch and was in the house.

He put the tool away and stood still in the kitchen. Soon his eyes adjusted to the dim light which filtered in through the windows.

The kitchen was as he remembered it, the hall still across from the rear entrance.

George walked carefully around the table and chairs, then made his way to the war-lover's hideous room.

The door was locked, and once more he used the bar to gain entrance.

The accouterments and 'trophies' of war populated the shelves.

George wrinkled his nose at the imagined scent of death. He shivered at the idea of the pain inflicted by the gathered items, and he felt sick to his stomach as he looked upon the skulls.

The skulls, barren of flesh and the spark which had made them men. Those were the items which had tripped him up the first time, years before. He had heard rumors of the grisly trophies through his father's rabid complaints to George's mother.

George took a deep breath, pulled an old, army duffel bag out from under his coat, and emptied the shelves.

It took him less than ten minutes; the half a dozen skulls were the last items in. He shook his head as he wrapped each one in a hand towel and tucked it away, safely. Soon he clipped the bag closed, slipped the strap over his shoulder and made his way out of the house.

He closed the back door behind him, stepped in his own prints and made for the woods once more. Later, a storm would move in, and snow would fall.

George could smell it in the air.

His tracks would be covered, and none would be the wiser for days, if not forever.

The war-lover had spoken to only a few people about his trophies.

And George doubted any of them would ask what happened to such wretched items.

George hummed to himself and headed home.

HIDING THEM AWAY

George's mother was passed out in his father's easy chair.

An empty bottle of wine stood on the coffee table. The television displayed the vertical bars of various colors.

She snored slightly, shifted in the chair, and let out some flatulence.

George paused, pulled the quilt off the couch and covered her up with it.

He didn't think she would ever recover from his father's death.

George left the television on and went into the basement. The entrance to the secret room was behind the oil tank. He pressed himself close to the granite foundation, slipped around the tank and slid the pocket-door back into the wall. With a final push, George was in the long room his father had built, a bunker in case of an atomic warfare. He flicked on the light.

Metal shelves lined the walls. His father's plan had been to stock them with non-perishable items, but cancer had cut all of his father's ideas and goals short.

George had found a better use for them.

Wooden boxes filled several of the shelving units. Each held war trophies George had stolen. Some came from museums. Others, from historical societies and libraries. Only a few originated from people's personal collections.

Those were the most dangerous to gather.

A painful lesson George had learned at the hands of the war-lover.

Part of George wanted to destroy the items, yet the act of destruction would, he felt, only pay homage to war itself.

And George wouldn't do such a thing.

Not ever.

The air in the room was warm, if somewhat stifled, and George shed his coat, hat and gloves. He dropped them on the bunk he occasionally slept in, and put the duffel bag down beside them.

As he looked at the bag, a wave of exhaustion spilled over him.

The letdown after the success of a venture.

George yawned and realized he needed sleep. He could empty the duffel bag in the morning. He glanced at the bunk, and then shook his head.

Mother will worry, he thought.

George stifled another yawn, left the room and turned off the light as he went.

In the morning, he would savor his victory.

He whistled to himself and made his way up the stairs to his bedroom.

His mother still snored in front of the silent television, ignorant of what her son had brought into the house.

A MORNING PICK-ME-UP

Joan woke up with the quilt on her, and a dull headache.

George is home, she thought, pushing herself up and out of the chair. She grimaced as the room tilted inappropriately. With a grunt, she kicked the cover away from her legs and staggered into the kitchen.

She got a pot of coffee going and a fresh bottle of cooking sherry out of the pantry. From the drying rack, she took her mug, added a healthy dose of the liquor to it and waited dully for the percolator to finish.

Jesus Christ, she thought, blinking at the sun streaming through the side door. *Why the hell does it have to be so damned bright out?*

A glance over at the table showed her George had already eaten breakfast.

All of yesterday's mail was organized, the table's Formica wiped down, and the newspaper neatly folded and placed in front of her chair.

She smiled at her son's small acts of kindness, and then she fought back tears.

George reminded her of his father.

After a few minutes, the coffee was ready, and she carried her mug to the table. A little splashed out and splattered her already stained house slippers, but she didn't care.

She wanted to read the news and to see what was happening in the world. Although she didn't think there'd be too much.

A quick glance at the front page of the *Portsmouth Herald* made her pause. John Boyd and his wife were dead.

Serves him right, Joan nodded. *Serves them both right. He didn't need to beat George the way he did. Didn't need to do it all, actually.*

She skimmed the rest of the paper, more focused on her coffee than on any news. The sherry took some of the edges off her headache, and she smiled.

George would be at the hospital. Such a sensitive boy who had to work as a janitor. She knew he should have been a musician or an artist, but those didn't pay, and George took care of her.

He's a good boy, she told herself. *A little free with other people's belongings. But, a good boy.*

Joan got to her feet, went to the coffeepot and added a little more, and a lot more sherry, to her mug. She looked at the bottle, lifted it and took a long drink.

The liquor was a balm as it settled in her stomach.

Better, she sighed. *Much better.*

Joan carried her drink into the front room, saw the television was off and turned it on. She fiddled with the antenna until she got NBC's *Today*, and returned to the safety and comfort of the easy chair.

She tried not to think of her husband and focused instead on the program. Vietnam was the main point, and she only listened with half an ear. Luckily for her, she didn't have to worry about George being drafted. He was a registered member of the Industrial Workers of the World, and no one would trust a Communist with a gun.

Not in America at least, she told herself.

The basement door rattled.

I thought he was at work. What's he doing downstairs? she thought.

The noise stopped.

"George?" she called over her shoulder.

He didn't answer.

Must be the wind, she thought, shaking her head. She finished her coffee and returned her attention to the television. A moment later, a commercial for the new Cadillac came on, and she forced herself out of the chair. There were a couple bottles of Wild Irish Rose wine beneath the sink, and she wanted to get one of them open.

The basement door shook in its frame.

Joan stiffened.

"George?" she asked.

A glance out the window showed motionless trees.

There was no wind.

"George, are you hurt?" she said. A horrific vision of George injured leaped into her mind, and she hurried to the basement door, which exploded as she neared it.

Wood flew everywhere, and a large panel slammed into her face. Joan reeled back from the impact, struck the back of a chair and fell down to her knees. She let out an involuntary scream as she looked down.

Blood poured out of her right knee from where two screws and part of a brass hinge had punched into the joint.

She tried to stand, but couldn't. Instead, she fell over onto her side, and another burst of pain ripped through her.

Her breath was ragged, and her vision became hazy.

Movement by the basement door caught her eye, and she turned her head to look.

A man stood there, headless. Dirty. Clad in a uniform. In his right hand, he held a long knife, and as he stepped into the kitchen, it seemed as though Joan could see through him.

She twisted around, ignored the pain and reached for the cabinet beneath the sink.

Something bright flashed, and blood exploded across the woodwork and the floor.

Her hand lay near her wrist, fingers still outstretched. Dark, crimson fluid seemed to shoot from her, and she realized, dully, how the blood surged with each pump of her heart.

Joan rolled onto her back and looked up.

The headless man was no longer headless.

He was a young Japanese man.

And he was angry.

Terribly angry.

He yelled questions at her in words she couldn't understand.

When she didn't answer, he snarled and drove his knife into her stomach.

Joan gasped; the pain was tremendous. She coughed, tasted blood, and looked down as he twisted the weapon in the wound.

She shrieked for so long her throat became raw, and she vomited blood.

The dead man withdrew his blade and looked at her. In a low tone, he asked her another question.

Joan could only shake her head.

She couldn't even speak.

His face became blank as he slightly lifted the knife.

Joan tried to scream again, but couldn't.

Not even as he cut off her other hand.

AFTER WORK

George was tired.

He had worked a double shift, and he hadn't been particularly enthused about it. Overtime couldn't be turned down, though, not when money was tight enough to begin with.

He stretched, hung his work coat up in his locker, put on his winter gear and grabbed his keys. Some of the other guys showered, but not George. He would clean up at home and not in front of others.

Of course, they had dates or the bowling league. A few would go off to the Masonic lodge.

George needed to take care of his mother. She wouldn't remember to eat. Some days she didn't even remember to shower. Hopefully, she hadn't wet herself again.

He sighed and pushed the thoughts away.

After he had closed the locker and secured it, he waved goodbye to the others and punched out. The walk to the parking lot was cold, the night air bitter and the sky clear. Above him, the stars shone brightly, their light joined by the half-moon.

George smiled, got into his father's old Pontiac and started the engine. Within a short time, he was on Route 1A and on his way home. He kept the radio off, turned up the heat and kept an eye out for black ice. The last thing he wanted was to end up like the war-lover and on a slab in the morgue.

I need to empty the bag, George told himself. He had slept late in the morning. The grisly war trophies and horrific memorabilia still remained jammed into the duffel. He stifled a yawn.

I'll make some coffee, he thought. *No work tomorrow. I can stay up late, get everything put away and maybe get Mom out of the house for a bit in the afternoon. Take her shopping for some new clothes. Maybe even go down into Nashua and catch a movie, if there's anything good playing.*

George nodded and smiled to himself. The plan was a good one.

Soon, he turned onto his street, passed through the yellow circles of light cast by the street lamps and pulled into his driveway.

All of the lights were off, but around the edges of the front room's shades, he caught the flicker of the television.

George sighed, shook his head and put the car into park. He turned off the engine, coughed and got out of the car. The cold snapped at him, and he hurried to the side door. As he let himself in, George paused.

A strong, familiar smell washed out of the kitchen. His nostrils flared as he tried to identify the scent, but he couldn't.

George stepped into the house and turned on the light.

The kitchen floor was covered in blood, splinters of wood, and his mother.

She had been butchered.

Her bloody clothes were in the sink along with her head, which seemed to be the biggest part of her.

George looked down and realized he was standing next to what looked to be her liver.

Numbly, he slowly closed the door and tried to make sense of what had happened.

But he couldn't.

There was no way to understand it.

What happened? he asked himself, looking around. "What happened?"

"You brought them here," his mother said.

George turned and looked to the front room.

His mother's voice had come from there. Just under the sound of the television.

He left the kitchen and went to sit on the couch.

His mother, or her ghost, sat in his father's chair.

She looked at him, her expression sad. In one hand, she held a glass of wine. The other, one of her Virginia Slim's. She hadn't smoked since his father had died.

"You're dead," George whispered.

His mother nodded. "I am. They killed me. Butchered me like a pig."

"Why?" George asked, then he shook his head. "Who?"

"Those Japanese you brought into the house," she said. "They're not happy. Not at all. I wish I knew what they wanted. Couldn't understand them, though. and they couldn't understand me."

"I…" George shook his head. "I didn't bring anyone into the house, Mom."

She looked at him sadly and sighed. "Yes you did, George. You went and stole again, last night."

George blushed.

"Don't deny it, George. I'm dead. Do you understand? *I'm dead!*" she yelled.

George winced.

She hardly ever yelled.

His mother took a sip of her wine, and then a pull on her cigarette. She exhaled odorless smoke and looked at him.

"You stole skulls out of Jonathan Boyd's house," she said accusingly.

George nodded.

"I assume they liked it there," his mother continued. "And when you took them, I think you upset them."

"Who?" George asked, feeling confused.

"The Japanese," she said patiently. "The Japanese. I saw their skulls, in the bag. Those were their skulls you stole. I don't think they're happy about it. Did you see the kitchen?"

"Yes," he whispered.

"Did you see me?" she asked.

George nodded.

"Now tell me honestly, George, after seeing all that, do you think they're happy?"

He shook his head. "What should I do, Mom?"

"I think you should get those skulls, and get them out of here," his mother answered. "I'm not sure what you're going to do about me, though."

"What do you mean?" he asked, frowning.

"George," she said gently, "I'm spread out all over the kitchen like a struck deer on the highway. What do you think the police are going to say when they see me?"

He straightened up.

"Oh no," he whispered.

She nodded. "Now, either get those skulls out of here then figure out what to do next, or just get out and run."

The television went dead, and the light in the kitchen went out.

George was alone in the darkness with the ghost of his mother.

She sighed.

"What?" he asked.

"I think it's too late now, George," she said.

"Too late for what?" he said, feeling his pulse begin to race.

"Too late for you to get out."

NOWHERE TO RUN

George heard footsteps on the basement stairs.

"Mom?" he whispered.

She didn't answer. She was gone.

George was alone in the house with his mother's dismembered corpse and the ghosts who had killed her.

The house, which would have been utterly familiar even in the darkness he now found himself in, became both menacing and terrifying.

The dead were coming for him.

George knew it.

He trembled as he got to his feet. His tongue ran along his lips nervously, and he swallowed convulsively.

I need to get out, he thought. *I need to get away from them.*

For a moment, he considered the side door. He would be closer to the car. Might even be able to get away with it.

Yet, to get there, he would have to pass through the kitchen, and the basement was too close.

The front door. Yes, he thought.

George hurried to the exit. The sensation of the cold steel of the knob against the palm of his hand sent a surge of joy through him. With a twist and a pull, he stepped over the threshold.

Instead of the cold January air, he felt the warmth of the house.

Horrified, George turned around, and walked into the closed front door.

Once more he grabbed the knob, twisted, pulled and left the house.

Only to find himself in the house again.

He couldn't get out.

The door only opened onto itself.

George started to hyperventilate.

He heard footsteps in the kitchen and the crash of what sounded like a chair against a wall.

Nothing was right.

Nothing.

George bumped into the wall, groped his way to the stairs and fell forward. He caught himself in time and scrambled up the worn, carpeted risers to the second floor.

He smelled the furnace and the oil tank.

He felt the chill of the basement around him as he realized he had gone down instead of up.

George turned around and found the smooth, round banister of the basement stairs.

No, no, no, he thought, moaning softly. George raced up the stairs and bumped into the granite walls of the basement.

I'm still downstairs! he screamed silently. *Oh, Jesus help me, I'm still down here!*

He groped along the walls, the stone piercingly cold beneath his flesh. George stumbled against boxes of long-forgotten clothes, old toys, and the detritus of his father's life.

George needed a place to hide.

Footsteps rang out on the wooden basement stairs.

His breath came in great, ragged bursts as he reached a corner, tried to push to his left and fell.

He fell for far longer than it should have taken for him to reach the floor.

When he finally landed, it wasn't on stone, but on blankets.

Light blinded him, and he rolled away.

After a moment, he opened his eyes and found himself in the fallout shelter behind the furnace.

The light was on.

Everything was as it should be, the duffel bag still on the bed.

George was on the bed.

He sat up slowly and listened.

Nothing.

George got off the bed.

He looked around.

Was it a nightmare? he asked himself. *Did I come down here and fall asleep after work?*

George looked down at himself and saw he was still in his work clothes.

A wave of relief washed over him.

"A nightmare," he whispered to himself. "Just a nightmare. Oh, thank God."

He walked to the pocket door. His mother would probably be passed out in the chair again, and he needed to check on her. She would have to eat. And he would have to draw a bath for her.

With a relieved sigh, he took hold of the pocket door and slid it back.

But it didn't budge.

It wouldn't move at all.

George tugged harder.

The door remained firmly closed.

Frowning, George began pulling on it fiercely.

Still it stayed in place.

What the hell? He thought.

Laughter burst out from the other side of the door.

The laughter of men.

Of several men.

George took a nervous step back. His heart rattled in his chest and with painful, jerky movements he sat down on the bed.

Fists pounded on the door. The laughter grew louder.

And the light in the room went out.

George was alone in the darkness.

TIME PASSES

He had no way to measure the time.

George didn't know if he had been in the fallout shelter for hours or for days, or simply, for minutes.

His stomach growled, yet each time it did, he thought of his mother, butchered and cast about the floor. The hunger passed.

George lay on his side on the bed. The duffel bag had been kicked onto the floor, and George was curled up under the old woolen Army surplus blanket. He was exhausted.

Whenever he dozed off, the dead knew it, and they pounded on the door.

He felt as though madness would consume him.

George was so terribly tired.

He just wanted to sleep.

Laughter penetrated the darkness and jarred him out of a doze.

They always know, he thought drunkenly. *How?*

George forced himself up from the bed.

A question came through the door, but he couldn't understand it.

"I don't speak Japanese!" he yelled. "Leave me alone!"

Fists hammered against the wood, and he jumped backward, slammed into a shelf and cried out.

A cold breath danced along the back of his neck, and George screamed.

The dead let out gleeful laughs.

Are they in here with me? he thought frantically.

Someone pulled on his ear, and George twisted around. "Stop it!"

The laughter stopped.

The light came on.

George closed his eyes and rubbed at them for a moment, but only a moment. He was too excited about the light.

He looked around the room.

Did they leave me alone? he wondered.

Silently he crept up to the door, took hold of the handle and cautiously pulled back on it.

It slid into the wall on silent runners.

And George found himself looking at, well, himself.

Another George stood in front of him. Behind the second George, was an identical fallout shelter. The new George wore the same stupefied expression, and George assumed he did as well.

It terrified him.

George and his curious twin both reached out and closed the pocket door.

He waited for his heart to stop its mad race within his chest, and then he slid the door open again.

Grey, cold granite greeted him.

George reached out and touched it.

The stone was real.

He pushed, and it resisted. He closed the door again, opened it, and found only stone.

George stared at it for a long minute, examined the time-worn marks from the quarry in the granite, and then he shut it out. He returned to the bed and collapsed onto it.

Slowly, he pulled himself into a fetal position, and he waited for something, anything to happen.

He didn't wait long.

The lights flickered, and then went out.

They're coming, George realized. They weren't going to wait any longer. They didn't want to return to the war-lover's house. No. He was sure of it.

They wanted him.

They wanted to hurt him.

The same way they had harmed his mother.

He would be butchered.

The door to the fallout shelter slid open, and they came in.

Their footsteps were loud on the floor, and he shivered at the sound of each one. His ears ached as he listened to them speak to one another softly in Japanese.

George heard knives drawn from sheaths.

He squeezed his eyes shut and chanted in a low whisper, "This isn't real. This isn't real. This isn't real."

The light came on, and George risked a glance.

Six headless men stood around the bed. They all wore uniforms. Each was khaki, yet some were filthy, others clean. Hatred and rage pulsed from the dead.

Two of them, George saw, had knives drawn. Terribly long knives. Short swords used for ritual suicide. Blades used to remove the head of an enemy.

The other four unarmed men pounced upon George, and as he screamed, they seized his arms and legs. Their grip was painful. Cold, needle-like pain punched through his wrists and ankles. George struggled, and the dead tightened their grasp on him.

With fury and fear, George fought to remain in a fetal position.

The dead would have none of it.

They stretched out his arms and legs and soon had him spread-eagle on the bed.

One of the knife-wielding ghosts leaned in and ever so neatly and cautiously, cut away George's clothing. Each piece went, the ghost's hands steady. No matter how much George writhed, he was not cut a single time.

It took only a few minutes, but soon George was naked on the bed, and he screamed furiously.

One of the dead spoke in Japanese, and the other five laughed cheerfully.

A hand reached out, grasped some of George's chest hair and pulled slowly.

George shrieked, more in outrage than from the pain. But he was terrified as he watched the skin slowly stretch as the hair was pulled farther up.

The dead man let go of his hair, made a remark and again they all laughed.

Then the laughter died down, and the ghosts who held his limbs tightened their grips.

George pictured his mother's remains, and he shook uncontrollably.

A moment later, he lost control of his bladder, and he wet himself.

Someone snorted in disgust.

George felt his hands and feet go numb, and the skin burned where the dead held him.

The two ghosts with knives stepped closer, and George closed his eyes.

At the first sharp bites of the steel, he screamed and bucked. He felt blood trickle out of the wounds they had made, and his heartbeat pounded in his ears as he listened to them speak.

"A fine mess you've made for yourself, isn't it?" a voice asked.

George opened his eyes, and he saw the war-lover.

The dead man, who wore a Marine Corps uniform, stood at the foot of the bed. All of the Japanese ghosts had their heads and looked respectfully at the war-lover.

"I'm not staying long," the war-lover said. "I was merely passing through. I heard the boys, though. Kind of hard to miss the Japanese, even in all the chatter out here. Not too many dead talking in anything other than English or French. Anyway, they're not happy. Just in case, you hadn't figured it out on your own."

"I'm sorry," George whispered. "Oh Jesus Christ, I'm *sorry!*"

"Don't doubt you are," the war-lover said unsympathetically. "Fact of the matter is, boy, I just don't care. This is your bed, literally as well as figuratively, so you may as well lie and die in it. They cut on your mother because they thought she was the one who had brought them here. Ichiru, here, is feeling mighty bad about doing it to the wrong person. I expect he's going to work just a little harder on you, now."

"But, I'm sorry," George whispered.

"I know," the war-lover said. "And they care about as much as I do."

Something flickered, and George looked in time to catch sight of the first knife plunging into his stomach.

The pain was excruciating.

* * *

Check out these best-selling series from our talented authors:

GHOST STORIES

RON RIPLEY
BERKLEY STREET SERIES
MOVING IN SERIES
HAUNTED COLLECTION SERIES
DEATH HUNTER SERIES

IAN FORTEY
JIGSAW OF SOULS SERIES
CULT OF THE ENDLESS NIGHT SERIES

SUPERNATURAL SUSPENSE

A. I. NASSER
SLAUGHTER SERIES
SIN SERIES

DAVID LONGHORN
NIGHTMARE SERIES
ASYLUM SERIES

SARA CLANCY
THE BELL WITCH SERIES
BANSHEE SERIES

For a complete list of our new releases and best-selling horror books, visit ScareStreet.com or scan the QR code below!

www.ingramcontent.com/pod-product-compliance
Lightning Source LLC
Chambersburg PA
CBHW050343030726
47503CB00008B/2591